indigo 33

a spooky novel
"Enlightening and thought provoking"
Literary Agent Quote.

Dr. Susan Phoenix

BALBOA.
PRESS
A DIVISION OF HAY HOUSE

Balboa Press books may be ordered through booksellers or by contacting:

Balboa Press
A Division of Hay House
1663 Liberty Drive
Bloomington, IN 47403
www.balboapress.com
1 (877) 407-4847

Because of the dynamic nature of the Internet, any web addresses or links contained in this book may have changed since publication and may no longer be valid. The views expressed in this work are solely those of the author and do not necessarily reflect the views of the publisher, and the publisher hereby disclaims any responsibility for them.

The author of this book does not dispense medical advice or prescribe the use of any technique as a form of treatment for physical, emotional, or medical problems without the advice of a physician, either directly or indirectly. The intent of the author is only to offer information of a general nature to help you in your quest for emotional and spiritual well-being. In the event you use any of the information in this book for yourself, which is your constitutional right, the author and the publisher assume no responsibility for your actions.

Any people depicted in stock imagery provided by Thinkstock are models, and such images are being used for illustrative purposes only. Certain stock imagery © Thinkstock.

Print information available on the last page.

ISBN: 978-1-5043-3942-1 (sc)
ISBN: 978-1-5043-3944-5 (hc)
ISBN: 978-1-5043-3943-8 (e)

Library of Congress Control Number: 2015913789

Balboa Press rev. date: 9/14/2015

Cover photograph courtesy of Marina Housley
(additional design by Redlinecompany.com)

This photograph was kindly provided by Marina Housley. The circumstances of its appearance are as intriguing as they are mysterious. She felt the spirits give her an almighty push whereby she was physically launched through a doorway by an unexplained force, which she took to signify the time to take the first step towards following her dream. The next morning she awoke to find this beautiful image of light energy spheres on her cell Phone.

We have taken the artistic liberty of adding some "ghostly" images in and around the spheres. One of which is my husband as we publish in the twenty first anniversary year of the Phoenix rising from his body on the beautiful Mull of kintyre.

I am so grateful to Marina for allowing me to use this special photograph that had given us such a lift, not least because it appeared at a time when I was struggling to finish Indigo 33.

Marina's story began with a fall or a 'push' and my book has been finished courtesy of a fall or a 'push' that broke my ribs, forcing me to sit down and finally put this book to bed. There is work to do in our world to encourage the positivity that can be found outside of the box that confines. Thank goodness for spirit orbs and cosmic pushes. If you don't believe me – prove me wrong, science and skeptics still cannot do that!

Enjoy the read … it's fiction but based very loosely on real life unexplainable 'stuff'.

Susan Phoenix 2015
www.susanphoenix.com

Comments about previous books by Susan :

quotes by readers of Out of the Shadows.:

from *Belfast News Letter* _

"Her story cannot fail to inspire hope in those who, like Susan, wonder where their life will go once it has been shattered. Perhaps it helps to have a name like Phoenix but 'Out of the Shadows' is proof that it is possible to rise up from the ashes once more."

from *Vickie Paget – Time 4 U magazine*:

"When I walked out into the busy embrace of the bracing fresh air outside Belfast's Europa Hotel, I felt decidedly odd …

But in a good way. A wee bit dizzy and dazed. A little bit shaky and light-footed. I feel a bit silly admitting this, but it was as if someone had tickled my heartstrings with soft, glittery fingertips.

'That's not something that happens every day!' I hear you cry, dear reader, and you're absolutely right - because it's not every day that you meet Susan Phoenix.

She's a very special lady indeed. She's taken life by the proverbials and squeezed every painful, joyful, crushing and exquisite emotion out of it – even the magical emotions. And if you ask me there's a lot more room for magical emotions in this world." … … … … …

This book is Susan's astonishingly personal contribution to all of those out there who are stumbling around in the dark trying to find a way to recover from trauma. The pages burst with the wise words of a wise woman who has been there before. And her fascinating journey continues …

'Atta girl …"
Spirit and Destiny Magasine journalist.

" … … Finished the book yesterday. It's such an incredible, intense and beautiful ending. Wow! A highly enjoyable book you've written there, and I think an important one because it's accessible to all and totally brings that whole magical world nicely down to earth. Well done."-

Readers quotes:

- " ... ... just wanted to say that I read your book - Out of the Shadows - in two days. It was a wonderful experience, a heart warming and mind-opening read."
- " ... ... You are one courageous lady, I'm impressed with your will power. Yours is a traumatic experience, deep sorrow, I was almost in tears when I read your piece in spirit and destiny. I didn't cry because I thought if this lady suffered this and came through it all there is hope for the world."
- "Your story has given me hope ... ...! Thank you for sharing your story, it must have taken great courage to share such a personal journey with the world ... ..."

For more information see:
www.susanphoenix.com

Dedication

This, my first novel, is written with love for my beautiful grand children may they always keep their inner wisdom to make magic, love and happiness in their lives.

Erin, Cian, Cora and Charlie.
Spain and England, 2015
In memory of all of their ancestors in those other dimensions

Summary

Georgina Griffiths was born with a special gift which she didn't fully understand until she started to study the science behind psychic phenomena. She had been reluctant to recognise her own supernatural powers despite the childhood presences—figures from other places and times who were desperate to communicate with her. As an adult, she retains weird memories of past lives.

When she met a group of believers in vibrational energy, things started to make sense. At last she knew that she was not crazy.

With a new perspective on the world around her and the support of her motley crew of friends, she published her PhD into angelic and spirit energy in the twenty first century. Some friends were living and others more etheric but she slowly realised that she already knew them from previous incarnations. Together they become the Indigo 33 group. What followed changed her life forever.

The globe spanning story features scenes from Welsh valleys to Miami Beach and onto the outer cosmos. The Indigos bring radical healing for unresolved past life experiences that encroach into this life, causing depression and drug addiction.

Working together, illustrating the science behind the myths, with a lot of earthy fun, they bridged all dimensions to bring healing to those in need. They were about to rock the world by producing previously suppressed evidence of their abilities.

They are about to rock the world as they produce scientific evidence for more than their own abilities.

Dr. Susan Phoenix - Author

Susan saw many spirits (known as ghosts) in her childhood. Her family terrace house was home to a Victorian lady complete with a bustle and a little girl with hair piled high. Unlike her heroine, Georgina, she grew out of it and did not see (or feel) anything else until her husband was killed. Feeling his spirit a few hours after his death lead her to research scientific papers about energy in the environment. Further research into complementary therapies and non-chemical help with grief and depression encouraged a new path in her life.

Since 1994 she has written two best selling non-fiction biographies (one, co-authored with Jack Holland). Indigo 33, her first novel, has been evolving over eight years as a result of her personal research into the world of clairvoyants, healers, energy medicine and psychic phenomena.

Susan Phoenix was a military nurse, youth worker and psychologist for deaf children in Northern Ireland until the death of her husband in an enigmatic helicopter crash on the Scottish Mull of Kintyre. In her quest for personal peace she moved first to France and then Spain before realising that all happiness and peace can be found inside of you. Her well grounded humour and tongue in cheek style earned her a reputation for no nonsense therapy in life. She now runs highly acclaimed inspirational workshops in past life regression, meditation, grief management and self-development, helping others to enjoy their life more by understanding the power of universal energy.

The Phoenix really did rise from the ashes.

Chapter 1

Introduction

It wasn't easy being Georgina.

She always felt older than her years; she always felt that she knew things before she was told. She had great difficulty staying in her body.

"How do you know that Jesus was thirty-three when he died?" black-haired Kyrie with the blue eyes, twinkling from under the curly fringe, asked.

"'Cause the Bible tells us so!" Georgina tossed her long, blonde hair over her shoulder as she sang her reply.

"What superstitious rubbish that is. It sounds more like a song title to me—you know the one we used to sing as kids? Yes, Jesus loves me, yes Jesus …"

"All right, Kyrie, shut up. Enough singing. But it is common knowledge that Jesus was crucified when he was thirty-three. I've always thought it to be a bit of a weird age for us too. You know, a sort of make-or-break time in life? Even you must have found that out, growing up in Belfast."

Kyrie gave a smirk and threw a red, lip-shaped cushion at her friend. Her black curls bobbed around her ears as she bounced into the linen-covered bucket chair beside the radiator. It was the favourite place for the girls to keep warm in the damp London winters. The Catholic girl from the Welsh valleys and the Northern Irish protestant had become firm friends when they had first met in the London gym, courtesy of

Kyrie's Welsh boyfriend, Eddie. They could tease each other about their differences and celebrate their similarities. Many hours were passed drinking cheap, teeth-blackening red wine, discussing their lives and lovers, on the well-worn settee in Kyrie's North London flat. Georgie went on to her favourite subject of looking for the synchronicities in life.,

She was used to her friends and relatives teasing and mocking her inherently held beliefs in "greater powers" from the universe. Her mother had often said, "There's something a bit weird about our Georgina," in a slightly proud but whimsical way. It was almost as if her mother wanted someone to agree with her and give all of the associated explanations as to why her youngest daughter seemed so different to her brothers.

Her gran remarked that when she was just a few weeks old, Georgina actually followed her surroundings with her intent gaze, quickly outgrowing those musical mobiles that hang over a baby's cot. Not for her a cylindrical, twirling, nonsensical toy. Her ears strained to hear the peripheral sounds from the garden and the outside environment. She could hear a bee droning through the old stone walls of her Welsh village home. She could feel the new energy of dawn before the curtains were opened each day. She really had no time to waste sleeping because there were things to see, hear, and learn. She was certain of that from her early days on Earth.

Her sleep patterns were erratic, and her little limbs wanted to be free to kick in her cot or push chair. She grew into a normal enough child, whatever the word *normal* means in our diverse society. Always underlying the normality of a little girl who loved to draw and write and be in her own quiet space was some kind of deep knowing, as though she were somehow older or more mature than her other family members. Her parents often expressed amazement at how she seemed to know facts about things that she could not possibly have learned from them or the village primary school to which she happily skipped off each day.

She just knew things that no ordinary child would even consider. It wasn't discussed outside the home, just seemingly accepted as "Georgina." They were not a particularly religious or academic family. They just got on with life, bringing up their children with kindness, discipline, and lots of real, unconditional love.

2

When she was about five or six, she started to have what the family called Georgie's nightmares. She would wake up screaming, her little body clutching at the bedding as sweat poured from the top of her thick blonde hair. Her heart was beating so loudly, she was sure it would burst from her tiny chest. The screams increased in volume and pitch for hours, sometimes for no apparent reason.

She would try to relate what she saw with stuttering words about strange figures with hoods and lanterns standing by her bed or animals running up the walls of the flower-papered bedroom. "Mam, I can hear them talking; don't know what they're saying. Sort of different voices, ladies and men and noises from the hills. Make them go away, please, mam."

"There, there, *cariad,* don't worry. There's nothing here to hurt you."

Her racing heartbeats and the clear visions in her head told her otherwise. Today the childcare books would tell her mother that Georgina was suffering from night terrors. Thirty years ago, it was not explained away by academics so easily. Her mother was trying to console herself as much as her daughter as together they glanced nervously around the shadowy bedroom.

If only someone had been able to tell them that she was just seeing the old connections with other lives and dimensions. Eventually her young mind tried to rationalise for herself what happened in the night. Sometimes the figures took more recognisable forms of old ladies and young Victorian girls. They took the time to smile at her and reassure her they would not harm or frighten her, if she could just try to focus and listen to them. It was this ability to focus that became her strength and her cross to bear, depending on which day she was considering her fate. There was, of course, also the support of her childhood friend Thomas. He had been a very good companion for a sensitive, young girl throughout those early years.

The conversation about Jesus was neither an unusual nor even a particularly spiritual one. The down-to-earth acceptance of subjects—factual, mystical, spiritual, and scientific—all in one brief chat with her new friends was one of the pleasures that she had at last come to realise. Her life had developed on a fast track from the friendly, smiling child in the village school, who had seemed studious but fun, to the dedicated scholar in grammar school and eventually to university, where she had been given free rein to feed her thirsty mind at last. Studying for a BA honours degree in theology and psychology was not her first choice, but it gave her an opportunity to read, reflect, and rationalise about what the world often called *weird*.

She still had the night time visits. She had told Kyrie about one boyfriend who ran screaming from her bed at about 4 a.m. as his dead granny tried to make herself known through Georgie's sleeping mouth. The old lady's spirit wanted so desperately to give a message from the other side to her daughter, the boy's mother, that she obviously thought the perfect opportunity was there pinned beside the wall in the single bed of the London University halls of residence, with sensitive Georgina a useful mouthpiece. Unable to wake her, the spirit from another dimension tried banging on the bed with enough energy to confuse even the best quantum physicist.

"Bloody hell, Georgie!" said the long-since-amorous boy, "when you said the Earth would move for us, I thought it would be something more physically sexy!"

Sleep-befuddled Georgina tried to reassure him. "Well, actually it is physical energy, but it just comes from beyond conventional physical boundaries as we know them, or rather as we are willing to believe them. Physicists talk about a line dividing our reality sharply in half—the event horizon."

"Some event!"

"I'm really sorry. I should've told you that I do seem to have been specialising in dead grannies recently, with the odd angel thrown in. If only I could do a doctorate in energies and angels, I would have a head start, but no one would believe me."

"Well I do now. So what about writing an outline for a PhD thesis to get you started?" he said excitedly, all sexual thoughts now transposed into an exotic idea that was to rock more than one boat. "Steven Spielberg, eat your heart out!"

Georgie didn't know it would be thirteen long years and that she would be thirty-three before she would find anyone to take her seriously. Had she known, she may have elected to go back to her home village right there and then to teach school like her brothers. She may even have hooked up with her childhood friend, Thomas, again.

Chapter 2

Thomas and Georgina

When Georgina was a child, she wanted to be a boy. In fact, she called herself George for months when at that pre-pubescent stage of life. She blamed the boyish name she had been given when yearning for more testosterone in her system. They called her a tomboy in the Welsh village where she grew up feeling safe to run the surrounding green fields with her brothers. The slate-roofed houses lining the narrow streets sheltered the children from the outside world. Warm fires belching smoke from the stone chimney stacks were still in evidence on most rooftops. Her glossy blonde locks were trapped into a single pigtail to aid the adventurous outdoor life that she craved. Later she discovered that her past-life memories had not been expunged at birth as was normal, and her most recent life had, in fact, been as a man.

As she matured into the esoteric journey that she had chosen in this lifetime many other strange facts were to become clear. Suffice to say, that in those early years boys were definitely perceived to have more "power" than girls. They got to do more interesting things than the stereotypical girl stuff that she despised. The boys in her family got to go fishing with Dad, ride motorbikes and do a lot of "clearing up outside" whilst girls were trained in the pursuit of domestic hygiene, inside the house, boring stuff that was complete anathema to a feisty young female who was raring to get on with life in the most physical ways possible. She found the household chores of washing dishes, dusting and polishing so unnecessary and turned into a sulky, droopy lipped teenager for several years, when asked to help with the cleaning.

If it had not been for Thomas she would have become a very bitter and twisted teenager. He had shared her desk in school from day one. She had been very annoyed when he had to move to allow another girl, Bronwen, to sit beside her. He had just smiled and moved graciously to one side, as he always did, in a sort of serene androgynous way. He looked like some kind of renaissance painting, soft auburn hair just skimming his ears, gentle blue eyes that looked into your soul and sparkled when he smiled or even when he was deep in thought. The skin over his cheeks looked almost translucent when he was resting, at times there was a glow of warmth that seemed to radiate from his whole body. She knew that Thomas was her best friend as he and Bronwen totally ignored each other, much to her childish pleasure.

Thomas had encouraged her to ask her dad if they could go along on some of the fishing trips to the fast flowing river that ran noisily through their village. It became a great source of pride that she became the best fly caster in the family. "She can cast for flippin miles- she can!" Her Dad proudly told the gentle and loving Mum at home. The fact that she also gained great pleasure from learning to tie flies with dexterity and flair probably contributed to her artistic talents in later years. She learned that sitting peacefully in her favourite crossed legged position, using beautiful feathers and turning them into something to attract the fish, contributed to her love of the outdoors and surviving from natural products. OK, so this was before the politically correct debate about the cruelty of fishing and whether the whole world should be organic vegetarians gained power. She knew that she caught her fish and helped them die quickly without obvious pain to eke out the family food stocks. Thomas told her that it was alright if the fish were for eating and thus helping the nitrogen cycle. The fact that time spent with her Dad and brothers in the peaceful countryside beside the river also gave her great pleasure seemed OK too.

It was Thomas who used to say that there was nothing so powerful as an idea whose time has come.

He said it was a quote from someone but she never remembered from where. When they had their finding out about life, pubescent discussions, she always reiterated the fact that so many books said the same things in different ways. Her argument that there was nothing new to be written about under the sun always met with strong argument from Thomas. He inevitably said the same thing – she thought it was boring but probably true. "It is not what you say but the way that you say it!" "Your time will come." He felt that different generations develop different abilities to perceive information in more positive ways. It was from him that she started to learn about theories of different universes and explanations as to why she seemed to have such an inherent inner knowing about so many things that astonished even her. He encouraged her to think outside the box and to internalise information that matched what was already developing in her eager young brain.

A telescope appeared one Christmas that contributed to their discussions. They would lie out under the stars in the old stone walled back garden and marvel at all they could see through the naked eye and then magnified thousands of times through the magic new instrument. They felt safe in the garden enclosed as it was with the dry stone walls built by another generation of Welsh crofters. The stones themselves reflected patterns from their original quarrying in the hills all around. They could feel the ancient energy when their childish hands caressed the beautiful cool rocks, seeking fossils compressed from countless millennia. She would close her eyes and feel herself being transported up into the sky with a light headed floating sensation. There were occasions when this floatiness turned into a whoosh of speed that had her clinging to Thomas for support. Together they rocketed up into the midst of galaxies through star gates (he said) and on into a peaceful plateau of vibrant colour that she would not see again until she learned to meditate properly as a young adult. That amazing peace to be found just by closing her eyes after a few minutes of stargazing was to help her many times in the years to come. At such times she knew that she could conquer the world. Quite how or when all that conquering would take place she had yet to work out.

It was wise Thomas who, forever full of quotes, said that your thoughts create your reality. He was always spouting off, ad nauseum, about your mind being more powerful than you know and that miracles seldom occurred in the lives of those who do not consider them possible.

Although she pretended to be bored by his pontificating she absorbed more information than she cared to admit. She thought an odd miracle wouldn't go amiss especially if it could encourage Thomas to kiss her one day soon.

When she forgot herself she would repeat some of these words of wisdom to her parents and they gave each other that odd, surprised and yet slightly fearful look. If she tried the same quotes with her brothers their reaction was always with eye rolling and gasps of "for Christ's sake Georgie, wise up and shut up!" No wonder they did not speak to Thomas, as far as they were concerned her head was full of enough nonsense and the sooner she got into sneaking out to apply makeup, tight jeans and to go to the local disco like her mates the better.

Dancing was not a pastime that attracted her and when she tired of the telescope she was happy having her chats with Thomas whose thought processes more than compensated for any musical diversion. Together they sped through the country lanes, bike wheels sizzling and sticking on the hot summer tarmac until they threw themselves down under a tree to rest, talk, sleep and talk some more. Often they had tennis rackets over their shoulders or fishing rods strapped along their bike frames to while away the long sunny days. They didn't waste time on those "what will you do when you leave school?" type of conversations. She had enough of that with school friends and her mothers' cosy pals who never knew what to say after "my how she is growing," casting about platitudes, assuming that they had nothing in common with young people. Georgie wanted to scream "I'm a person, just like you so let's have real chat about the meaning of life and death, all those things you are too scared to address to anyone. I wanna KNOW!"

"Do you know what is out there in this Universe of ours; do you suddenly wise up and get massive revelations of information when you reach a certain age?"

"How is it I often feel that I have met someone before, why do you look as though I have known you somewhere else?"

"Can you look into a friend's eyes and see what is going on inside?";

"When do you get to understand that other person's needs by just a chat, is it honest or what?"

"Is there a colour surrounding someone that changes as they get older?"

"Do you see those great colours that I see when I look at a stranger? It's really cool just looking. Sort of like a halo that glows?"

"Is it Ok for me to talk about dead people and that I seem to know when someone is about to die? Don't you know that I see their energy change around them, I see their eyes lose that power for maybe a few days before they go. Wish I could tell people this."

"Do you see this or am I really weird like my brothers say?"

"Oh yes and I know what Mam's making for dinner before I get home is that strange or what?" "Sometimes I even think my Mam was my sister somewhere else and my Dad was my son?"

"You know I have had dreams that feel so real, I was reading a book about the French Pyrenees in school and I am sure the pages dissolved and I was in the pictures wearing long old fashioned clothes and an apron. I could smell something like the rosemary and sage that Mam grows in our garden here. Weird eh?"

Thomas didn't think it weird or strange at all.

They loved their bike rides no matter at what time of the year. The winter roads made the mud splash up from the bike wheels so that her Mum often remarked that she looked like a farmer fresh from mucking out the pigs as she arrived, glowing pink cheeked, muddied and energised at the kitchen door on chilly November evenings. Winter nights were for reading, devouring any book she could find as she fed her hungry mind to try and catch up to the intellectual heights of Thomas. She loved the cosiness in the warm sitting room as the patterns from the coal fire danced around the walls.

In fact it had been a coal miner, sitting on her family sofa, who had told her how upset he had been when the local mine had closed down.

"Mind you I didn't miss the choking black dust in my nose and tubes like, the cave ins and even ruddy explosions, you know?"

Thomas asked him where he had lived ;

"Well, here, bach, right here in this cottage, 'cause it is a wee bit bigger now and the floor was built up a bit so I s'pose you can't see my feet nowadays?" At this both Georgie and Thomas looked downwards to realise that their visitor did appear to be chopped off at mid-calf level.

9

The sooty faced figure raised his hands in supplication and grinned as he too looked downwards.

"Aye, it was a sad day for us all when the work dried up. Funny 'cos I had become friendly with an old Roman fella who had been working the coal away back then, you know, when Ancient Rome needed the black stuff?"

"What happened to him?"

"Come to think of it I'm not sure, I only used to meet him in one of the longer seams, took me a while to realise he was long dead, 'cause my mates never saw him. Spooky it was. He used to work in a sort of leather apron, a loin cloth type of thing, when I come to think on it. Wondered why they started to call me 'Mad Matt' if I mentioned him, Atilius he was called, handsome big lad, shiny dark brown skin!" Matt smiled at the memory and then suddenly shot up straight in his seat. "Gawd, I guess that means I'm the same as him now don't it? I wonder where he is now, flipping heck maybe I'll see him again eh?"

"He will have passed over eventually and is probably already occupying another body."

Georgie and Mad Matt both turned to look at Thomas as he made this pronouncement.

Was she really having this conversation or was she dreaming?

Her sleepy gaze was pulled from the pages of her book to the flames creating volcanic leaping wall shadows and the depths of the fire grate produced hot red caverns of stalactites and stalagmites as the wood and coal merged into pure heat energy.

Maybe she should study physics.

As the light improved in springtime she took up her sketchpad and reproduced credible likenesses of friends and family. She also drew exotic landscapes reminiscent of the Middle East, that she had only seen in books, minarets in distant villages approached from desert tracks, camels looking incredibly lifelike. Many doodles on the edge of her note books had hieroglyphics all intertwined along their margins. Those landscapes morphed into North American Indian plains with migrating tribes of Indians, soon to be called first nation people, on horseback disappearing into horizons of fir trees and snow capped mountains. Here, spiralled petroglyphs decorated rocks around the edges of her notes as she doodled over the paper whilst dreaming her way through the evenings, listening to the old fashioned dance music that her parents loved.

Maybe she should study art.

How was it that in her early teens she felt so proud of her Dad's ability to do usefully constructive stuff in the house such as that fitted kitchen, perfectly moulded to the crooked stone walls, only to feel ashamed that they did not have a new sleeker television like her school pals just a few short months later. Everything was relative she discovered.

Her shame was short lived when Thomas helped her to talk through such materialistic thinking. Those friends who had the smart television in its new stages of digital sophistication, well they had a cumbersome piece of kit in their homes that really did nothing for their eyes or their décor. It had moved on a lot since the early developments by Logi Baird who tamed the airwaves to send moving pictures in the nineteen twenties. Sixty years on Thomas and Georgie were still not impressed that the invasion of their atmospheric energy had been suitably tamed to replace their love of books.

Maybe she should study literature.

Books and paintings filled their days and their sponge like brains. Dreams with realistic scenarios encompassing people past, present and unknown images filled Georgina's sleeping head. Were they recorded in hard wiring into her brain or did they linger in an as yet undiscovered mind? Was her mind the same as her brain and where did the soul come into all of this? Such subliminal discussions she had with herself, rarely daring to broach such subjects with any of her peers. The ever helpful Thomas of course, was the dependable cerebral wall to bounce her ideas against. He was also good at answering questions with another question –

"you should've been a detective!" she said.

"I was" came the reply.

"Yeah right, Inspector Morse!"

"You'll understand much more one day."

She did not doubt that with his help, she would.

Chapter 3

Kyrie

"Jesus, Mary and Joseph what have you done?"

"For God's sake will you stop talking like a religious maniac just because you're Irish?" I wouldn't mind but you're not even catholic."

"Ok, ok, but just tell me how you got yourself beaten up." Eddie was looking chalky white and sweaty around the gills with blood running from his nose, bypassing his thin taut mouth and dripping onto his once white Hugo Boss T shirt.

"No one touched me, it just started after I took my last snort. It's never happened before. Am I dying? Fuck, I think I'm dying!" he panicked.

At this stage, Kyrie could not say as she had never seen anything like it before, although she had flirted around the edge of the fast living, drinking, and drug using set since she hit London in her late teens. This had been her escape from a narrow judgmental life in Northern Ireland when the troubles had been in full swing, over twenty years ago. Looking at her ex boyfriend now she felt as though she were back in the petrol bomb throwing back streets of her home town.

"Jesus" she said again to buy herself some time before she could get a grasp of the situation. "Sit down you stupid shit we'll have to get you a doctor 'cos that is really thick blood. It could be a brain haemorrhage for all I know." She was getting a damp cloth from the kitchen after pushing him roughly into the battered bucket chair that had seen too many greasy heads and TV dinners. Luckily, for them both, their pal Giles chose this moment to arrive with his usual flourish without knocking on the half open door. He was so shocked he didn't even do his usual "when is a door a jar" joke. "Oh Gawd, too much of the white stuff elegant Eddie? When will you learn?"

"How do you know?" asked Kyrie almost admiringly.

"Typical after such abuse to the old nasal cavity sweetie, he is lucky it didn't happen before, knowing his history of trying to fly without wings" At this he leaned into Eddie's face and gave him one of the penetrating gazes that no one could avoid. Soul searching was a perfect description of Giles' eyes.

"How much did you take?"

"Half a gram."

"Well if you are going to tell me lies I'm off – when are you going to be honest with yourself, never mind us!"

"Sorry, yes, oh shit, it was a celebration gram, you're right. I only took it 'cause I got a job and it was to be my last, honest!"

"Believe that and you'll believe anything" Giles winked across at Kyrie, "I think you should ring the doctor and the police and see can we sort this prat out once and for all"

Eddie shot out of the chair and threw himself at Giles pleading and crying "NO, don't, you can't I'll lose the job before I even start!" The resultant shuffling dance with Giles trying to avoid blood stains on his own neatly ironed linen shirt looked almost comical.

Kyrie was standing watching this little scene wondering how she had got into such a place from her so called God fearing community at home. Her mother with the Queen's picture on the wall and a bible beside the bed would turn in her grave if she had one – but she didn't because she had been burned and scattered beside her beloved Lough. It was the Welsh Catholic boyfriend who had brought her to the big smoke, together, escaping a life that was eating their happiness if not their souls. He had been the catholic soldier, bemused by his role in the peace keeping of a "foreign" land where everyone supposedly spoke his language and yet seemed to understand nothing of what he said. She had been the small town protestant girl who was not supposed to even speak to "the other side" according to her family's intransigent rules.

The fact that Eddie was a Welsh soldier made no difference when the family started their religious arguments with bigotry borne of long forgotten grievances.

Not for Kyrie and Eddie the bitterness and bewilderment of under educated peers trying to taunt at best and kill each other at worst. They knew that there was another life for them where they could love who and what they wanted without ignorant judgement and recrimination. Their love affair didn't last, of course, but it had been enough to help them jump out of the airless box that was Belfast in those troubled days. They were mature enough to know that their relationship had been a "for just a season" and a practical arrangement that did not need to be the lifetime stuff that filled romantic novels of their era. Twenty years on from that exodus, they often quoted that saying about friendship being for "a reason, a season or a lifetime" when they wanted to explain their evolved friendship.

Eddie had been a handsome young Welshman, and ex squaddie from the Welsh Guards, who had introduced her to Georgina, another Welsh exile at their gym. He had initially taken to spliff smoking and then graduated to class A drugs as he tried to find his feet in the civilian world of London. Friends joked that when the Irish met the Welsh anything could happen. In the case of blond haired Georgina and dark curly mopped Kyrie it was instant friendship with a mutual respect leading to a reciprocal sharing of new ideas. They left it to the guys to do the hard drinking, scuffling that passed for fights and later the drug taking. It was Eddie's eventual love of getting a hit on cocaine that led to the split from Kyrie. She was not averse to losing the odd day from alcohol but drew the line at mind altering drugs that cost a fortune for a short fix. She could just about cope with her hangovers but did not want to mess with the few brain cells she suspected she had left. In fact, once she got to know Georgina, who was ten years her junior, she really wished that she had not screwed with her brain quite so much.

With Georgina's friendship she started to see that there were more things that she could do if she kept sober for longer. She even started to process information so that not only could she remember it but develop her knowledge onto higher levels of understanding. In fact she often related to her work pals that it had been "fucking amazing" to wake

14

up one day without a hangover and realise that she was actually feeling excited about reading a new book about energy medicine. "I mean I didn't even read my O level course books but this is fascinating!" She had enjoyed teasing the younger Georgina about her spooky ideas but quietly took on board some of the less weird concepts that she could understand. The books about energy and vibrations made sense to her as she slowly allowed her undereducated brain to catch up with her life experience.

The particular level of understanding called for in the scene unfolding in front of her now was one she wished she could just by pass. Giles had managed to calm Eddie and stem the flow of blood with a cold damp cloth on his nose. They were in deep conversation about rehab units, narcotics anonymous, alcoholics anonymous and the need to "get a grip" in one way or another. The internet had been a great source of help and support to Giles when his partner Ralph had been thrown from his massive motor bike once too often as a result of too many JDs (Jack Daniels). He had become something of an expert on all manner of self help groups, 12 step programmes and whatever it took to get Ralph dry and clean for the past 5 years. He often said that there is nothing worse than a convert as Ralph spouted off about the demon drink during their many parties in one house or another. No matter, it had worked and their relationship had been saved and blossomed into an almost Darby and Joan style of love now. They were still party animals but Ralph could cope with the lemonades and various caffeine laced fizzy drinks without alcohol. Giles continued to sip his classic dry martinis in his usual rather genteel manner. Right now he was being less genteel as he tried to get his point across to Eddie.

A thought struck Kyrie that perhaps Georgina could help out with some form of energy healing for Eddie to give him some strength and will power back. She opened her mouth before engaging her brain and suggested just that. The two men turned to look at her, as one, with derision and laughter all over their faces.

"What?"

"Don't talk rubbish!"

"Now Kyrie dear, this is something that calls for professional intervention from qualified medical practitioners and people who know what they are doing."

"Yeah not some form of mumbo jumbo with no scientific basis whatsoever!" A new bravado from Eddie as the blood had stopped flowing down his chin.

"How do you know it is no help Giles, when come to think of it, Ralph enjoyed his sessions with Georgina a few months back?"

"Ah well, yes, but that was just a little relaxation technique that she taught him, nothing as heavy as this. It certainly did no harm but he could have listened to some soothing music while I rubbed his feet and got the same effect." He turned to Eddie again in a womanly confiding manner, "his blood pressure was sky high and the doctor wanted to give him even more drugs, so he needed to learn other techniques you see?"

"You two really piss me off, you have no idea about what she does and condemn without even trying or being willing to try."

"I know she talks about spirits and I prefer mine out of a bottle, thank you very much!" Eddie was regaining some pin pricks of colour into his white cheeks as the panic in his voice subsided.

With a renewed confidence, Eddie was forgetting that his dependency went further than just the white stuff. His first vodka in the afternoon had been getting earlier each day, just passing time until he thought it was Ok to go in search of his first hit of the early evening. He was also enjoying the bit of male bonding with Giles in spite of his early resistance to Kyrie's gay friends. "I mean they might make a pass at me!" he had said prior to the first meeting. "You should be so lucky!" was Kyrie's dry response. Neither his small town Welsh upbringing nor the military training had really prepared him for all the spontaneous "coming out" that happened in the big smoke. The Scottish moor's glorious twelfth had nothing on the splendid plumage of the gay scene in those early days. Not that elegant Giles or biker Ralph approved of many of their peers who they often described as "as camp as a row of tents dearie!"

Kyrie was already phoning Georgina whilst ignoring what she called the flat earth ignorant comments of her friends.

"No he isn't asking for help, the blood has stopped flowing now." She was half whispering into the mobile phone.

"No, I don't think he really wants to deal with his problems."

"Well Ok but if you get a chance will you drop over for a cuppa later?"

As she crooned "byee" down the phone she turned to Eddie thoughtfully.

"She says she'll send you some light and healing but unless you ask for help she can't interfere as the Universal Laws may have other plans for you."

"What the hell does that mean then? Ah right, that's it then I'm obviously doomed – what does she mean she can't help me, for fuck sake?"

"Well you said you didn't want her 'cos you think it's all baloney anyway."

Eddie's tone turned to a wheedling little boy voice, "Yes, well, but I might just like to try a wee bit of her energy stuff, just for relaxing you know like Ralph, come on cariad, see can you get her over then I will think about one of these groups that Giles seems to be a world expert on."

She was trying hard not to grin triumphantly as she picked up the phone to her psychic friend who was already, anyway, tuning into Eddie's soul group in another dimension.

The energies from other dimensions were also tuning into the small sitting room where another of life's little miracles was starting to unfold.

17

Chapter 4

Georgina the Psychic

Tuning in to the other dimensions was a regular occurrence for Georgina now, but remembering to switch off and come back into her body after these sessions was proving to be difficult for someone who just loved to have the cosmic freedom that the ether provided. She often thought of those wonderful night skies that she had shared with Thomas and her Christmas telescope. How simple life had seemed then. She missed his guidance and wise words more than she realised. She had lost touch when she came to the city to do her first degree. Her Phd research was almost finished, She had eventually managed to find an academic supervisor who had helped her register the doctoral thesis covering Angels and Energies in the twenty first century. She was enjoying living in halls of residence again with none of the problems associated with renting a bedsit or sharing friends's flats that had accompanied he earlier days of studying in London. Flatmates had never quite understood her night time ramblings and invisible "visitors" who chose to impart knowledge to her sleeping soul at inconvenient hours. Now in her own single room she could relax and take time to meditate in peace as she put the finishing touches to her thesis.

Listening to Kyrie on the phone had brought a real buzzing into her scalp. This familiar sensation told her that she had work to do and the Universe was sending appropriate energies to help her. It was an odd understanding that she was forming with the spiritual and angelic hierarchy almost without any motivation on her part she often felt drawn into situations that called for her special gifts. And yet still she wondered why. She had been questioning herself on a number of occasions when she knew that she had helped someone out of a stressful situation. But was it a personal ego trip? After all she wasn't Mother Teresa was she? Is this why the old mystics and saints who took Holy orders said that they had been called to work for God? These kind of statements had always made her feel uneasy and more than a little embarrassed. Who did those saintly types think they were anyway and why did they feel that they had some kind of superior power? Many of these questions came to her when she had briefly tried to learn from her elders in a spiritual Church in the town near to her home village.

Over ten years ago, as a teenager and before escaping Wales, at about the same time that Kyrie and her own Welsh lover were crossing the Irish Sea, she had felt the need to learn more about the spiritual energies that entered her bedroom at night. As a very small child she had been terrified and it was Thomas who had been the first friend to help her understand that she need not be afraid. When she was very small he had sat beside her bed, when she was sleeping, and asked the amazing shapes and flimsy edged people to just go away and not come back until Georgina was older and able to communicate with them. He never told her, of course, that he had been able to communicate so easily with the spirit world. He just knew that she was not ready to see them until she was around ten or eleven. It took her some time to accept that she could really see what others could not. Her school friend Bronwen, who had shoved Thomas so rudely from his seat beside Georgina in the village school, seemed to accept her friend's odd behaviour without needing to ask too many questions. She felt very blessed to have such accepting pals.

In those early years the fact that some disembodied souls were waving at her from behind the person with whom she was chatting was a tad disconcerting. She would be enjoying a chat with a friend or acquaintance when an energy from from another plane would start to materialise behind the friend in front of her. This was usually a very real looking slightly wispy edged body with facial expressions indicating that they had a message for her to give the other person. Sometimes, if she knew the friend well she would ask whether they would they like to hear what their spirit friend wanted to say. This was always a bit of a chance to take as it could make people do a variety of things. Some would actually run away, muttering "looper" or "mad witch". Others would ask who it was and others would just immediately say "yes please, go ahead, tell me all!" in an excited and welcoming manner.

Bronwen liked to recount the day she was standing beside her friend Georgina chatting to an elderly neighbour in the narrow village street. The two fifteen year old girls were lounging against the old stone wall that enclosed the church yard, the slate roofed church dwarfing the arched gateway that opened into the grassy graveyard behind them. It was one of those breezy spring days with an unusually blue sky being tickled by wispy clouds as they floated high above the surrounding hill tops. Georgina and Bronwen had often roamed the green fields that ran down the slopes from the craggy top of their favourite mountain nearby. They had picked bluebells and cowslips in the spring sunshine and sheltered from the sudden rain showers in the broken down shepherds hut below the torrs. The egg sandwiches made by their Mams always contained salad cream and sometimes a bit of gelatinous laver bread left over from breakfast. But here now was the elderly Mrs Edwards asking them if they would like to call and get some fresh laver bread that she had just left cooling in her kitchen.

"Freshly made it is, cariad, I boiled the laver for an hour before rolling it in our wheaten oats and frying in the best bacon fat you ever tasted."

Georgina choked with laughter as she said "stop it now, away with you, for God's sake!"

Bronwen and Mrs Edwards were flabbergasted as they looked at Georgina, she was never known to be cheeky, odd yes, but never cheeky.

"No seriously stop it!" Georgina appeared to be looking, in a slightly drunken way, over Mrs Edwards's stooped tweed clad shoulder. Bronwen decided it was time to nudge her pal into some kind of manners. She did one of those sideways glances children give as they dig an elbow into each other. She shoved her head and neck forwards as she poked her hard in the ribs.

"Georgie !"

Georgina pulled herself back into her body and her eyes cleared in time to look more sensibly at Bronwen.

"What is it?"

"Well my girl, you could just have said if you didn't fancy a bit of fresh baking, no need to be so rude!"

"No I am so sorry Mrs Edwards, I wasn't talking to you, really I wasn't. I got a wee bit diverted. You see there is a guy over there called William and he says he never liked the way you rolled the oats with an old milk bottle. He was always a bit suspicious in case the bottle had been out on the front step." Bronwen pushed herself away from the churchyard wall in time to catch Mrs Edwards as she slipped towards the tarmac.

"Georgie!"

"What? I'm sorry I didn't think, just got carried away he looks so real and he was making me laugh. Are you Ok Mrs Edwards?"

Bronwen was trying to balance the tiny white faced woman on her not insubstantial thigh. She had dragged her towards the wall and was making a makeshift seat using her thigh and the wall for stability. Luckily Mrs Edwards was as slight in stature as Bronwen was sturdy with strong thighs honed by the local harriers running club. "I'm sorry, she normally lets me know first before she starts talking to the other world in public Mrs E, are you Ok now?"

"You really did see him then, didn't you?" The tweed coat was now dragging on the floor as the woman slumped gratefully against Bronwen. Bronwen was almost squatting now as she too sank further down against the old granite stones that had almost certainly been witnessing such scenes on the other side of the wall, beside the gravestones, for many centuries.

"Do you think we could shift to the tea shop across the road where Mrs E can sit down properly for a minute Georgie?" Bronwen was raising her eyebrows and trying to nod as she jerked her head towards her aching knee to get the urgency of this request across to Georgina. She realised that the shocked woman was beyond sensitivity to the pain in her thigh by now.

"No, no cariad I'm fine now just a bit of a shock that was all. Here's me going on about food when all the time our William is standing beside me and I never even knew." Mrs Edwards jumped up like a youngster as she allowed the adrenaline of the situation to fill her body. She felt an enormous surge of happy energy and smiled like a cheshire cat. "Tell me Georgina did he look OK, was he happy, is he still here and can you still see him?" Love and excitement filled the space around the three of them as they hugged each other spontaneously.

"Oh dear me, Mrs E, I am so sorry to have just come out with it like that and thank you so much for being so understanding, I usually get more warning and control my reactions but he was so funny and so powerful with his energy I just had to answer him immediately. Please tell me you're not frightened or anything?"

Mrs Edwards gave her another hug as she said, "You've no idea how much that meant to me Georgina, you couldn't know but our William was killed in a climbing accident many years ago when he was a young man, I have always wanted a sign or a message from him and I never thought it would come like this." Now relieved of her slightly built passenger, Bronwen leaned back to take a deep breath, and slid her foot up the wall behind her to stretch the muscle of her leg. Georgina was looking around her to check if there was anyone there who still needed to send any thoughts over. She was secretly thrilled to be able to openly communicate with the other dimensions and the irony of it being beside the grave yard was not lost on her young mind.

"O, Oh, here we go again!" Bronwen was watching that glazed, dreamy effect come over her friend's eyes as Mrs Edwards, too decided that she needed the support of the old granite wall behind her back.

"He's saying 33, he was 33 … Glencoe … should've listened to his Da … snow came too quick. Oh I can feel tumbling dizziness, did he fall or … no he was covered. I can see the white snow shining now. He said it was beautiful, just white snow, then white light … Oh that is lovely." Georgina's eyes were shining with happiness now and it looked as though she were in a completely different space to this narrow village street beside the church. The tears were streaming down the older woman's face and she too was smiling with a painful happiness that only the bereaved can know.

"Yes he went in November to Glencoe with some of his pals from Northern Ireland, they went every year, but that season there had been too many avalanches and his dad told him to wait till spring. You know young men, they always know best and his friends were all skilled climbers, just like himself. Is he Ok now ?" Bronwen was nodding at her with an eye on Georgina to see when she was coming back into her body. There was more to say and the two of them focussed once more on Georgina's voice.

"He says to let you know that he is around whenever you need him and he hears you sending love to him. He likes the candles that you light, but less of the smelly ones, they make him sneeze and frighten the cat!" Georgina laughed out loud here too and nodded as she acknowledged the spirit communication even more, her words continued, oblivious to her surroundings. "He has been at peace over there for a long time now and is happy that you don't cry so much now. Yes, I see." She was nodding again at her invisible narrator and holding her chest as though in pain, "you have to look after that chest and make sure you get enough exercise, he says, your heart is fine it has just been the stress of loss and worry, stop it now OK? You were wondering whether to take the tablets the doctor wanted you to have, but you're right to trust your self, no statins ! Wow he is very strong about this, yes I see alright I get it no, no thank you I *am* telling her. He says his dad agrees with him." She turned to look at Mrs Edwards,

"Gosh he is really strong willed isn't he? I can feel his personality right here." She tapped her forehead as she said this and then shook her head as if to clear some of William's energy field from her own.

"He was always a powerful force to be reckoned with. Him and his Da had many a skirmish over just about everything in the house. I was relieved when he went off to work in Scotland, have to say, it was hard for him to be an adult where he had been a boy, understandable, I know but ..." Here she drifted off to think about the past again as Georgina appeared to lift her eyes to the heavens without moving her head.

"Right, ok now I get it, hello is this you ? Oh I see, your Dad is here, thank you, I understand yes." Mrs Edwards jumped away from the wall as if she too could see her husband, she wished that she could climb in behind Georgina's eyes.

"Dr Edwards, yes I remember you when I was little," She started to cough in a deep raucous way that did not sound like a 15 year old girl at all.

"Oh! Right, he's showing me his lungs all black and, oh so yucky!"

"He died from lung cancer, knew he shouldn't smoke, but all those years of study. when we had no money he was in medical school ... for ever it seemed." Mrs Edwards interjected and was really focussing now trying to get every bit of information that came from Georgina's lips.

"William met him when he passed over, wants to thank you for stroking his hand all that last night in the hospice, he felt your love, oh yes and he still feels it. He is sorry he had to go, but he likes what you're doing for the hospice now. They need you he says, it will keep you young, maybe even love again!"

Mrs Edwards nearly choked through her renewed tears at this comment, "Well I never, at my age!" Georgina was nodding again now, "Right I'll tell her, thank you and no, I know, it was an honour for me too. Good bye be happy too, thank you."

With that last reverential nod Georgina appeared to drop back into her body from goodness knows where and her eyes refocussed on her friend and the older woman. Both were drenched in tears and holding hands like long lost friends.

"Oh my." gasped Mrs Edwards as she hugged them both all over again with such a force that they were all pinned to the church yard wall. The local bus chose this time to come through the narrow gap that was the road between church and the tea shop on the opposite pavement. The sound of the horn made all three jump and push themselves towards the arched gateway. As Bronwen pushed the wooden gate open to sink onto the grass just inside she wondered why they hadn't done this 30 minutes ago.

Georgina wandered off amongst the grave stones to try to re centre herself. She had not known what would happen after that first giggling glimpse of the disembodied William over his mother's shoulder. Her energy levels were now quite low and she really needed to get a drink and something to eat to ground herself back into her body.

Bronwen was sitting with her arm round the still slightly bemused Mrs Edwards who had flopped down beside her on the grass at the side of the gravel path leading past the graves to the church door some 200 yards away. "And to think I was only offering some laver bread!"

"You can say that again, I have never seen her say so much, I am gobsmacked to say the least. Did it all feel true to you then? You see she never really has faith in what she sees."

Mrs Edwards was smiling again in that far off way as if she was in a private space from years ago. Nostalgia bringing the past into the present. "You know our William always went on about my using the milk bottle to roll out my baking. He even bought me a beautiful new ceramic rolling pin, but I just preferred the way my Mam did it. There's no way that anyone else knew that and it was such a comfort to know he didn't panic when the snow covered them, didn't it sound lovely cariad, you know when she said it went from white snow to white light? I can see him going off instantly can't you?" Bronwen nodded encouragingly and squeezed the tweed clad shoulders a little tighter. "I always wondered if his dad would find him when he went too. It was just a few years after, I thought my world had ended all together, but knowing he went earlier so that he could help his dad at the end, well that's such a comfort, oh yes." A little sob came out if her lips as she covered them with her tiny bird like hand. Bronwen was thinking that if laver bread helped you stay slim like this dainty lady then she would get her Mam to make loads.

Georgina was meandering back through the larger tombstones around the church. She stopped at one and patted the old carved stone with her pale hand. She flicked her long blond hair back as she stood beside the tomb. Mrs Edwards looked over and called out, "That's the Edwards family tomb, village doctors for generations. Never thought William would be there before his dad, but now I know they are not in there either. It's funny how bodies are no good to us in the end no matter how we primp and preen in our life. My goodness what a morning I have had."

"Yep, Mrs E you had better be getting home to do some primping and preening right now, never know when that new love is coming along do you?" She received a playful punch on her arm for this as she started to haul the seventy year old up from the fresh green grass. Another hug to Bronwen and Mrs Edwards almost jogged over to give Georgina a farewell hug with even more thanks. "I really can't thank you enough. Now do not neglect that gift of yours cariad it is really a blessing to be used to help many more people than me, I am sure." She patted her husband and son's tombstone as she turned and walked briskly out of the slated archway that led to the street once more. She really needed to go home and spend some time with her thoughts in peace. She would remember this day for the rest of her life.

Georgina was wandering thoughtfully back to where Bronwen leaned against the old stone pillars supporting the gateway.

"Well I didn't see that coming at all, well done, very impressive."

"Oh Bron I shouldn't have done it like that, all out of the blue with no warning to poor Mrs Edwards, I could've terrified her."

"Well you didn't, she loved it, it was real therapy if you ask me. I've never seen her look so happy, ecstatic I would say actually."

"Thanks for that, but I really do have to get a grip and learn more about what I am supposed to do with all of this don't you think?"

"Well I'm not so sure that you need help that was really amazing, like something off the telly. I've seen those psychic shows and I am sure they couldn't do it any better than you just did there on the side of the blooming road for God's sake!"

But Georgina knew that she needed help and support to deal with this odd gift that could easily become a burden.

Looking for guidance she went along to the small unassuming building that was the local spiritual church. It almost felt clandestine in those days as she slipped in the side door to join the motley crew of the congregation. There was a kindly faced middle aged man on the platform addressing the group in what she discovered was the standard format for such services. They always started with some prayers and asked for spirit energy to be with them and for the protection of the light. It seemed like a regular Christian church with some silk flowers along the edge of the rostrum. Candles fluttered in the atmosphere in a welcoming way giving off a rich glow to the wooden balustrades along the front of the hall.

A few people had nodded at her in a welcoming way as she edged into her chair half way along the row. It didn't feel too threatening and she started to think that this was going to be a big help in her new life on her way to University a few years later. As she settled into her seat she began to relax and allow her gaze to wander around the other members. There were anorak clad men and women with plastic carrier bags at their feet, perhaps on their way home from shopping. She was not surprised to see other people dressed in their Sunday best as was the norm in her Mum's parish church most weekends. She was surprised to see all age groups from teenage to elderly, as very few youngsters went along to her parish church any more. The young had long ago found more interesting diversion than listening to some old duffer spout off about sin and damnation. They could not imagine what those rather dusty looking preachers could possibly tell them about their life. (In fact they didn't even know that they were on a life path.) No the teenagers in her small town were more interested in pure unadulterated hedonism perhaps because their grand parents had survived the war, their own parents did not like to give them too many rules and regulations to curtail their enjoyment of life.

So what was there here for her in this assorted group of individuals? The committee members were a close and defensive group who guarded their regular church membership like a secret society. Indeed it wasn't too many years earlier when such committed "spiritualists" had been forced to meet in darkened rooms in secret locations with fear of being arrested for black magic or some such trumped up charge. One of the grey haired ladies had told Georgina about her younger days when they used secret signs to let other spiritualists know where the next weekly meeting would be. "We still called them séances in those days and they were very into materialising matter. You know, getting a spirit to appear in the room, lots of bumping tables and moving a glass around to match letters for messages. There was a lot of trance mediumship and the like. We would meet in darkened rooms with the curtains drawn and even leave a look-out for the police in the street. Yes, hard to believe now but we could be arrested for even believing in spirit energy. We were always being accused of calling up the dead. Load of nonsense of course, but you know what fear will do to common sense. The traditional churches spread even more fear by denying spirit and even some of them banned angels can you imagine that ?" Georgina found it hard to imagine such clandestine groups from as recently as the the mid years of her own century.

The angels and disembodied spirits in this spiritual church were already chuckling at such ignorance. If only the world knew how it really was. Now in more widely accepted "churches", as the weekly services were underway, there would be "readings" from the stage.

"I have a John here in spirit can anyone take this? I am feeling a pain in my chest, he could have died from a heart attack."

"I am seeing a hospital bed and lots of tubes - he is telling me that he was relieved to pass over at the end there had been too much suffering. He thanks you for sponging his lips during that last night, he was really thirsty. He wants you to know he loves you very much."

This was the format of so many messages that came from the spirit world to the expectant congregation. As the bereaved person smiled, cried or just looked numb Georgina could see their departed family member standing beside them willing the medium no the stage to tell them some thing more. It was obvious to Georgina that they wanted to comfort the living person and let them know that they were ticking over very well in that other world of energy without a human body. Some of the mediums who came to the stage were skilled and could see the spiritual energy standing beside their loved ones, just as Georgina could. These mediums would continue to offer information until the spirit started to fade away. If their loved one in the congregation was really receptive they could actually feel an energy field around them and love crossed the dimensions to give even more physical comfort. These were the most satisfying interactions for all concerned. She could easily see, however, that some of the so called clairvoyants and mediums were just complete bluffers, and they played straight into the hands of the cynics. There could be no doubt that they were enjoying their own importance being on the stage.

"I have someone with a letter A in their name. Can anyone take this?"

She searched the faces of desperate people who so wanted it to be a message for them. Once a lead was taken they tried so hard to make it fit what they wanted to hear and so did the bluffer on stage.

"Yes A, is it Andrew, Anne or maybe Angus?"

This was just too many questions for Georgina who could already see the spiritual energy flapping arms like wings to illustrate that her name had been Angela – of course! (Like an Angel). She knew this because she herself was often given an image or a conceptual depiction of something that the passed over soul wanted her to understand. When she actually heard the name, as she had with Mrs Edward's William, without the need for graphic visualisations, she always said a quiet "thank you" under her breath.

She had been aware that the church committee members sat at the back of the congregation, some looking quite terrifying. The closed body language, crossed arms and legs with many frowning faces, of all shapes and sizes, could be quite daunting for a visiting medium doing their thing from the podium. Georgina once described them as the bovver boys of the committee, lacking only the fashionable bovver boots favoured by hard men in the village to complete the intimidation. It was at one of these meetings that she first realised that not everyone who supposedly worked "with the light" as she liked to think of the special energies that she had been able to see glowing at her from a very young age, was in fact doing it for the good of society or the individual. She was shocked at the end of one meeting to be approached by someone who purported to be an elder of the spiritual group and see real anger in the woman's eyes directed at herself. The dowdy woman, mousey hair scraped into an unflattering bun, was clutching a beige cardigan to he scrawny chest.

"When one of the church elders gives a message from the stage there is no reason for you to add more information later you know. In fact it is considered very bad form to do so!" The heavily veined hands were clutching at the elbows of the cardigan as her crossed arms protected the low energy heart chakra from escaping into the world.

"Oh, I'm sorry but I thought anything that helped the person to get as much information from the other side as possible was valuable for them!"

"That maybe so, but not if it makes the person on the stage look inadequate!" The pursed lips of the older woman left no doubt as to how she felt about this attractive young interloper.

This was a concept that had never occurred to Georgina, who only ever thought about the needs of those who were receiving her messages. She focused on whether they were hoping for more or sometimes no information at all from a departed loved one. Her instinct told her that a message was usually welcome but only if that person was in the right mental space themselves. Some grieving or needy people were like sponges and took on board whatever their spirit friend wanted them to know. Others, she had discovered were like rocks that all the water in the world could drip onto but never permeate. When the student is ready the teacher appears, they say, but if the teacher is in the form of an invisible entity she already knew that great caution is needed.

At this moment she was not sure whether the woman in front of her with the glaring anger was a teacher for her or just a jealous demon sent to taunt. Had she really been too naive, she thought?

"I am really sorry, I would never want to do that but maybe you could help me to learn how best to give messages, I really want to learn how to do it properly."

"It takes many years of experience to reach a level that is acceptable you know. I am not sure that you are ready to join us here, we are a very elite group and I will have to put your name forward for consideration if you want to join one of our development groups. You have so much to learn." The frumpy middle aged woman simpered at the teenage Georgina. Her tight smile didn't reach her eyes as they assessed the tight blue jeans and pretty skinny top of her would be pupil. "We'll really have to see my dear, don't get your hopes up, most of our members are older and have a real gift." Georgina muttered her embarrassed thanks and walked towards the door. The older woman called to her as she went, "It would be a good idea to tie all that hair up out of the way if you want to be taken seriously in this business!" Georgina hung her head to hide her blushing face behind the glorious weight of shiny blond hair.

The real teacher from this scenario appeared in the local coffee shop, later, in the form of her old school friend Bronwen, she had just related the whole story of the church elder and was wondering whether she should just forget the whole mediumship idea.

"Surely you recognise a jealous ole bitch when you see one?"

Until this time she really had not been aware of jealousy directed towards her from anyone, given the loving family and direct speaking friends, who told it as it was, without malice. The additional message that she had learned here was just how lucky she had been. She whispered another of her quiet little "thank you's" as she smiled gratefully at her out spoken friend.

"Do you know I also saw the Chairperson of the church paying the visiting speaker with a whole pile of pennies and loose coins from the collection as she left. I mean you would think they could be a bit more sophisticated than that. How embarrassing and demeaning to have to fill your bag like that after a morning's work of spreading the light."

"Yep, sort of pennies from heaven I suppose." Bronwen added with a giggle as she sipped her large skinny latte.

Georgina had been so bemused by this payment happening in the public foyer that she hadn't even noticed the angel sitting in the hallway as she left the wannabe church. He nodded to another energy form that was draped around the door sending out as many positive thoughts as he could. The spirit guide, Eoin, was about to become more involved in his earth bound mission. She shuddered as she felt the air move around her but she had been too upset to see what had caused the movement in her energy field.

It had been the time to grow up for Georgina.

The more worldly and very supportive Bronwen knew exactly what advice to finish with,

"Time to grow a pair Georgie girl! You can show them all."

Chapter 5

Eoin

As a spirit guide, Eoin loves to translate esoteric stories for all of those who are still confined to earthbound bodies and have limited vibration in their cognitive functions. He liked to wax lyrical and was aware he needed to tone it down a bit. He, too, was once in a human body and had found it quite frustrating at times. For that reason he liked to drop in on his old friends to provide regular recaps and graphic imagery to keep them up to speed, in the picture, on the same page and whatever other new age expression considered in vogue at the time. When he last went through earth school it became increasingly difficult to deal with the combined physical and spiritual prejudicial limits that the twenty and twenty first century had imposed on earth's culture. He had been happier in earlier centuries when real people did real things to survive. They had lived close to nature away back then and the seasons dictated lifestyle and occupations. In this century it was frustrating for him when watching joyous souls float out of their bodies during meditation only to see them being sucked back into needy, almost concrete masses of flesh that instantly re focused on the next Prada handbag, Bugatti car or Chopard wrist watch.

He often lamented to any passing spiritual entities, "How is that so many humans think getting out of their body in meditation once a day is enough of a trip to allow them to do whatever else turns them on, even if it hurts others ?" He was unaware that he looked like a camp version of a grounded saint because he loved to materialise in an assortment of outfits from different centuries and different roles. It was his idea of defying stereotypes and not being pigeonholed by anyone tuned in enough to the other dimensions to actually see him.

He had a tendency to moan at any disembodied souls or angelic beings who would listen; "I mean, look at them, as they try the next spiritual fad, it's just like the old fashioned regular church goer who confessed their daft, perceived, sins and then did it all over again the next day. What DO they think they're at eh?" On this particular day he had materialised across the Atlantic in a rather smart Ocean view apartment in Miami's South Beach. He never knew why he was in a certain location until it all became obvious. He was *the watcher* before he was *the guide*.

Eoin watched the young woman, already getting settled into the dining room. With her hippy head band and crystal ball she prepared to look interestingly spooky and give psychic readings to a group of people in an elegant condo block right on Ocean Drive in Miami Beach. You know the sort of place, it could be a sea front anywhere in the world? It is where you can meet a microcosm of the world's wealthy, not so wealthy and assorted evacuees from the colder northern climes. They are the snow birds or "birds in golden cages." He had been joined by Archangel Jophiel and Ramese, junior angel in apprenticeship, under Jophiel's guidance.

Eoin was pontificating for the benefit of Ramese. "These are the ladies who sit along any warm coast seeking diversion with their husbands' platinum cards in their Gucci bags. You meet them in places like Florida, Spain, Mexico, Cannes and you can think of many more, I know. They are easy prey for the spoofers in the miscellaneous peripheral "professions." Just as the lonely older guys with a healthy bank balance fall prey to the imported lady escorts, from places as far afield as Thailand and Russia, so do their female counterparts attract the clairvoyants, assorted counsellors, massage therapists, life coaches and other nebulous professionals. Not that there are not some very professional and ethical therapists, of course, but I do so worry about the vulnerability of these lonely souls."

This was the all encompassing, over generalising description that the now slightly bored looking angels were hearing from Eoin as they floated ethereally together in a companionable way in this particular Miami home. If they were solid mass they would have been nudging each other in their non existent ribs about now. Spirit guides like Eoin and Angels like Jophiel enjoyed their pan American trips just as much as earthbound souls. No crowded airports or rough seas for the inter dimensional energies who could chose when, where and how to visit who ever may need them. Not that everyone knew that they needed such help, naturally.

Eoin was chuckling away to himself as he heard a discussion about www. One of the stylish young women was chatting to her friend over a chilled glass of sauvignon whilst waiting for a personal reading with spooky Juanita. "You do know the meaning of www. Don't you?"

"Of course I do it is world wide web!"

"Not any more it's not. I heard the best translation yesterday. Around here it stands for wrinkly wealthy willies.!"

The explosion of giggles was really entertaining Eoin as he made a mental note to tell this one to another of his pals from the angelic realms. "Remember, Jophiel, you heard it here first!" Angels really do enjoy a good joke that's why they are able to fly so well, because they take themselves and others lightly.

Eoin and Jophiel settled themselves on the rather grand chandelier, causing the crystal droplets to vibrate slightly as they prepared to eaves drop some more. Eoin had already warned young Ramese not to waft too much energy in the direction of the more pouty woman, he was concerned that she would stick like a sink plunger directly onto the ormolu mirror or patio doors if she happened to fall against a smooth surface. "You never know with those trout pouts!" Ramese looked towards Jophiel in shocked disbelief at this comment. The more experienced archangel smiled benignly and shook his head, having heard more outrageous statements from his friend Eoin on many occasions.

The girls went on to discuss which of their wealthy benefactors was paying for their meeting with this clairvoyant today.

"My Wesley says she is probably a con artist with a crystal ball like he used to see in the fairgrounds when he was a kid in Ohio but I told him it was worth a try." Her own mid west American accent added to the multi cultural feel in the room. Her cockney friend who looked like a million dollars, until she opened her mouth, was also being funded by an elderly Jeremy, another man who liked to be seen with suitable arm candy. She had found that her American friends expected English girls to speak like Eliza Doolittle and they loved listening to her chat. In fact she had tuned up her accent since she hit Florida. She was, after all, known for being obliging to all who knew her.

"Oh I know, Jer said something similar and I have an open mind really. He just wants me to have fun and spend his money wisely, he says, so who am I to be tight with his cash?"

The English blonde with the well filled pouty lips took another sip of her wine and crossed her legs decorously.

"Do you think she will tell us that we are going to be rich and marry a prince or what?" The almost identically sculpted lips of her friend continued; "Wesley says that there are so many charlatans around here right now that I should be careful, but it's just a bit of fun anyway, your Jeremy is so generous though, lucky girl."

Both girls pouted and puffed up their shoulders to squeeze their new silicone enhanced cleavages, almost like two budgies breasting each other for a bizarre fluffed up courtship.

"Yes, I know I am grateful, but he is pushing eighty and definitely comes into that www category." They both exploded with giggles once more as they rocked back into the plush cream leather sofas. "I heard that this Juanita is some kind of a Shaman and tarot card reader from Ecuador, or one of those hot places away down South. Have you met her before?" Eoin was getting really agitated now as Jophiel was consulting his automatic downloads that entered his energy field from the akashic records so that he could check Universal facts about anyone's lives in any century, anywhere in the world. Jophiel was shaking his head to such an extent that his glowing silver halo was spinning like an antenna.

"I don't need you to tell me dear boy, that our Juanita, here is definitely part of the charlatan group. Oh yes, I know, that she is not long out of Ecuador, she looks the part, of course, most of the hoaxers seem to adopt this same kind of attire. The gypsy look has not really disappeared since – well, since those early black and white films from

Ireland and Latin America made it look sexy and mystic. Oh dearie me, yes I know." Eoin was beckoning to the junior angel Ramese, who had floated over to join the fun, as he continued. "If you want to seem spiritual and mystical on earth today it is usual to bring in the long floaty velvet dresses, jingly bracelets, ear rings, the odd crystal or two et voila you have the look. But how can we help the average punter sort the chaff from the wheat so to speak?"

Ramese was blending his energy field with Jophiel to have his own look at the Akashics, a sort of universal, etheric supercomputer that he, as a junior Angel had really not learned to look at properly never mind download into his consciousness.

"I love the way you angels can do that sort of reading over the shoulder trick, with knowledge based downloads. I really must have a go some day when I am feeling really tuned in." Both angels were now shaking their heads causing their glowing halos to intertwine slightly like Olympic rings.

"She was not allocated any special insight or clairvoyant abilities in this lifetime at all:" As he said this Jophiel appeared to twitch his neck at such an angle that Ramese, suddenly unhooked from the halo link, spun off into the room looking worried in an angelic sort of blustering sparkling energy ball.

"Gosh, careful my friends, spectacular fireworks there." Eoin glanced towards the young women on the sofa but they seemed oblivious as they were now well into their second, oversized glass of sauvignon. "So, just as we thought, she has no super powers or even a special gift. It is so sad when there is so much to do, but I suspect that poor little Juanita had not been given much choice, she knew she needed to get out of Ecuador in her teens and was determined not to take the route of paid flesh that several of her girl friends used to escape their poverty. If she just had some spiritual education she could use her intuition and perhaps be more credible." Jophiel replied to Eoin's outburst by heaving such a sad sigh that he ruffled his own feathers and swung the chandelier several feet on it's chain.

"Mind you, the male versions of Juanita can be just as bad. Have you seen the guys who feel the need to wear Nehru shirts, or T shirts with an ohm symbol or some such identifiable spiritual sign on a leather thong around their necks. I mean, if these 'free spirits' had been asked to wear a uniform they would have refused but they did anyway." Jophiel was nodding with enthusiasm now although knowing that he was not supposed to sit in judgement, sometimes it was hard. He agreed with Eoin as neither of them liked stereotypes. The fact that Eoin was wearing his own version of a safari hunting outfit today seemed irrelevant to them both.

"Have you heard the expression- If you want to be a bear be a grizzly – I think that is human warrior speak for going over the top in style? These people certainly do that. The Juanitas of this world are really dedicated to making money and many do believe that they have the "gift" or the "vision." Occasionally they hit the nail on the head and give out information that can be supportive and even uplifting to a suffering soul. Nothing wrong with that. Rather that than a box of medically prescribed tranquillisers, I'm sure."

Eoin's pontifications were interrupted by Juanita appearing in the doorway from the dining room to invite the next client to cross her palm with silver. The first client came out dripping with tears provoked by the earlier reading that had taken place whilst the three spiritual energies were viewing the two blondes in the sitting room, stroke, waiting room. The next eager participant gave the tearful woman leaving a quick hug and went into the dining room. Eoin glided noiselessly in behind the elderly client who had just arrived without joining the pouters on the sofa. He was hoping to give her some support if he could get into her energy field to strengthen her personal space. He immediately took in the atmosphere that Juanita had created in the dining room of the luxury apartment. The sitting room, with the cream sofas had been transformed into a makeshift waiting room, full of light and objet d'arts assembled by the imported interior designer whilst the dining room naturally became the consultation area. In the darkened dining room there were incense sticks burning and the shiny crystal ball was sitting on the table with a stack of well thumbed tarot cards beside it. The table had been covered with the statutory deep purple velvet cloth. Several candles glimmered around the room designed to give a cosy glow to Juanita's sallow skin. The husky South American voice wasted no time in getting started.

"That will be feefty dollars pleez, just to get us started and then I can pop eet out of the way." The handy silver box with Indian engravings was also on the table for just that purpose of holding and hiding the fee.

"Now tell me your name pleez and where you were born."

"I am Wilhelmina Cross and I was born in Vancouver over fifty years ago now, Ok seventy years." Wilhelmina decided to be honest as Juanita had raised her eyebrows at the slight frugality with the numbers initially given.

"Oh yes and I am widowed from Jimmy these past ten years."

This early bonus for Juanita to hear about a dead spouse was most welcome. In fact Juanita was good at getting information by raising these darkly pencilled eyebrows. Her lashes were thick and mascara laden whilst the whole rim of each eye was blackened with a thick line of kohl pencil. Her lustrous dark hair was pinned up at one side with an ornate hair slide in the shape of a colourful butterfly on her purple headband.

"You see Ramese? How I wish that I could warn people to raise suspicions if they have spent a lot of time answering questions before they begin a reading with a tarot card reader". The young angel had appeared through the wall to learn more from the esteemed spirit guide that Eoin was known to be. He already knew that a lot of information is gleaned in this way and he was learning that a clever intuitive can build on this personal knowledge to tell the client what they, themselves, had just related for them. The fact that he could learn from Eoin, with a lot of humour involved, added to his experience, once he had cleared the unconventional style with his Archangel tutor.

"You see she just repeats a lot of the earlier facts back to the client that she has already given away herself.?" Ramese grinned appreciatively and hovered closer to Juanita. "Good guess that a woman in her seventies would have a deceased father don't you think?"

Juanita gazed deeply into her crystal ball, her piercing eyes could frighten a cat if it were passing. She closed her eyes momentarily as she looked up once more.

"Ah, I see you have a father in the spirit who has not been able to pass over properly – they are TRAPPED- yes trapped I FEEL heez distress." Wilhelmina started to look uncomfortable and shifted in her chair to see if her father could be felt around her.

"You see?" Eoin was looking so smug at this and he winked at Ramese.

Juanita had raised her arms dramatically as though to encompass the energy of the whole room. Her head went backwards and she closed her eyes once more as she spoke.

"I can help heem to find heez peace on the other side – you have come to see me just in time- he need thees help so much!"

"Gawd! Heaven help us !" Muttered Eoin, as Ramese appeared to choke on the ether that made up his present materialisation, visible only to Eoin and Jophiel, who was still enjoying the pouty conversations next door. Wilhelmina was looking aghast at this outburst, holding firmly to the arms of the ornate dining carver chair, keeping her head very still, she turned her eyes from side to side seeking whatever or whoever was giving this information to Juanita.

"Oh dear, how do you know this? Is there something that I can do? Maybe it is my Jimmy and not my father at all."

"Watch this, it's priceless!" Eoin spluttered at Ramese, whilst trying to also attract Jophiel's attention through the wall. Juanita was working hard on the Canadian matron in her dramatic, throaty Latino accent with great flourishing arm movements within what looked like a trance-like state. "No, no eez your papa. He tells me that he is in distress, Dios mio, it will take me such a lot of time and energy to free this poor trapped soul. I will need another one hundred dollars to do thees work!" Wilhelmina had not noticed that one of Juanita's eyes had surreptitiously opened to check the effect her performance was having on her client.

"Honestly, It's enough to make your deceased relative come back to get the bank loan for the journey!!" Scoffed Eoin. "Pockets in shrouds and all that stuff!"

He was whispering into the shocked client`s ear now, "Don't listen, it's a con, get out now, it's all about money!" Eoin then tried to blow into her hair and work on her physical feelings as he didn't seem to be able to reach her soul energy. "Come on, do some wing flapping Ramese, don't just float there, this is really bad."

Wilhelmina was starting to think for herself, having smelled a rat with this performance, although not entirely sure. She was after all a straight speaking Vancouver wife and mother who had not suffered fools gladly in her married life. She missed her man so much in her new life here in the sunshine. It was only for that reason that she thought she would give this psychic stuff a try. Now she was starting to have misgivings, knowing her widow's pension could only stretch so far, spirituality was one thing but greedy charlatans were another she was thinking. The room suddenly filled with a whoosh of air that caused Juanita to open both eyes very quickly. Jophiel appeared from a great height accompanied by another spirit energy who was looking a little windswept. His full head of pure white wavy hair, lumber jack shirt and hiking boots gave a tough Canadian energy to the room.

"Great idea, Jophiel, go to work Jimmy." Eoin had immediately realised that the handsome newcomer was Wilhelmina's long dead husband, brought by Jophiel to see could he get into her electromagnetic field more quickly. In the inter dimensional spirit world introductions were rarely necessary as everyone was automatically part of the greater Universal energy and resulting group consciousness.

The three spirit energies floated ceiling-wards to give the loving energy field that was Jimmy a chance to operate on his old soul mate. All three sighed "AWH!" as he carefully blended his love into Wilhelmina's soul energy. She automatically closed her eyes and sighed in unison as she felt the love and positive energy from her husband's soul. He was whispering subconsciously into her mind and she actually thought she heard something. Juanita was narrowing her eyes and swivelling her head on her slim brown neck as she wondered what was happening. She had certainly felt the air change but did not understand how her client had seemingly dropped into a trance state without any influence from her.

"Oh yes" breathed Wilhelmina with an even deep sigh, "thank you so much, I love you too."

"What? Who are you talking wiz? What eez happening lady? I did not tell you anything like zat!" Juanita was really starting to fret now, peering first into her crystal ball then shuffling her cards and eventually fanning herself with an incense stick as she crossed herself with fast jerky hand movements.

Several minutes later Wilhelmina opened her eyes dreamily and looked across at the now furiously bemused Juanita. "It looks like I won't be needing your help anymore today Signorita. Thank you anyway. I have had a lovely chat with my husband and he says to let you know that you have a lot to learn."

Juanita really loved a good horror story and this scenario did not fit into her repertoire at all. She seemed to be fascinated with dark energy and often told the client that she could see a dark energy around them when they sat down. For the dark effect she had always relied upon her voice that came across as deep and sexy as a result of smoking too many cheroots almost since she could walk. One of her mother's many "uncles" had thought it cute to sit her tiny toddler body barefoot on the bar with a cheroot in her hand. So this idea of some great un seen love that had just surrounded her client was really throwing her off course.

Immune to Juanita's performance, and full of Jimmy's love energy even the angels were getting excited to such an extent that the chandelier and candle flames were moving with their combined etheric energies. Eoin was hovering very close to Juanita now and appeared to be shouting in her ear.

"Ah see silly girl ? Jimmy dear boy that was wonderful, I do hope that you will stay in contact with your wife a little more often now that she knows you're around?"

Jophiel, having drifted off to watch the waiting room again, was chatting casually through the wall as though he were in the same room, which technically speaking or quantum physically speaking he was. "I too am very impressed and thank you for coming at such short notice Jimmy, my downloads had told me that you had never made contact with your wife since you came over, it was long overdue I think."

Jimmy's rich Canadian accent filled both rooms as he said "I had not wanted to bother her as we were very much a no nonsense, down to earth family (pardon the pun) and I did not for one minute think she would believe in any of this stuff. I certainly didn't till I passed over. We weren't even religious, just rites of passage church goers, you know weddings, funerals and the like?"

Eoin and the angels were nodding wisely in agreement. Eoin called to Jimmy's energy field as it was already drifting towards the ceiling. "Don't leave it so long next time, I think she may be about to join a meditation class with a little yoga on the beach thrown in for good measure. She would value your input once she gets that under way I am certain."

They had missed the hasty exit that Wilhelmina made from the dining room. She had shaken her head at the blondes on her way out. She really just wanted to find somewhere quiet to digest what had happened to her in that darkened room. She knew it was nothing or maybe something to do with Juanita but had some quiet analysis to do. The blonde girls by now seemed quite unconcerned by anything more spiritual than wondering whether there was any brandy in the drinks cabinet.

"Voila, Ramese, It normally takes a very strong person to leave such a session and decide that it really was all a pantomime. The doubt seed has been sown and the discontented soul needs to find some balance to feel happy again. Luckily our favourite Archangel knew exactly who to bring in to save the day. You can see though that we have a big job to do, don't we ?"

Eoin always wanted to follow the distressed client and guide them towards a genuine spirit medium who could put their minds at rest. Sometimes they got lucky and today Wilhelmina had struck the jackpot with her immediate acceptance of the message. Her intuition was kicking into gear and she would be rewarded in the months to come as she learned more about herself in the meditation and yoga groups that would suddenly become available to her. Jimmy was already trying to work out how to flick leaflets in front of her as she visited the local libraries and information centres.

Ramese and Eoin were still discussing what they could do to discourage Juanita from cheating vulnerable people. How different it could have been had they not been able to get the positive message of love with Jimmy's spirit. On this occasion Eoin had to content himself by blowing into Juanita's face whenever possible and nudging her cards onto the floor at all opportunities. It made her shiver and do that exaggerated crossing of herself that Latinos love to do. The downside of these tactics is that she really started to believe her own publicity as a clairvoyant extraordinaire.

Still Eoin vowed to research more exotic ways of scaring her as often as possible. He knew only too well that she had not seen or felt the real power of their combined energy in the room and that was enough to illustrate that she was no clairvoyant at all. He had already spotted her open diary on a side table. It concerned him that she had noted a spiritual meeting in a country house in England for gifted healers, mediums and clairvoyants. "She must be getting well paid for this fiasco stuff if she can afford to go over to Europe for a meeting. We need to let a few of our friends know about this interloper, methinks!" He knew that many of his friends and spirit contacts would be attending the noted gathering. Perhaps they would be able to help her to see that her guesswork and acting ability that focussed only on gaining income from the vulnerable, was not sufficiently developed to do this kind of work. In fact with great concentration he flipped the diary onto the floor in disgust.

His friends in the angelic realms were not very pleased with him when they saw that he was going overboard in the haunting area.

"I do wish he wouldn't do that!" Said Jophiel as he settled back down on the over stuffed sofa to listen to more of the pouty girls' chat. What do they say "vengeance is mine" sayeth the Lord? "Depends who's Lord and which day it is and whether you are religiously inclined and what you believe in. Or not! The loud tutting from his angelic pals did not stop Eoin's perverse pleasure in trying to put this little witch in her place!

"Come along gentlemen we have some serious work to do if we want to discourage such inadequate superstitiousness being mistaken for paranormal belief. We have a challenging project although not so daunting when the new spiritual science will be made clear. Up and away!"

All three energy fields ascended into the atmosphere, leaving the trouty pouters shivering and Juanita's room somewhat of a mess.

Ah Juanita! What have you done?

There is a can of worms about to open.

There could be trouble ahead.

Chapter 6

Lyre

Doctor Lyre Papakostas had not married in this lifetime, her mission statement or life remit had called for more dedication to her work than a family would have allowed. She trained as a medical doctor in London and Greece supported by a wealthy family.

Her unborn soul had chosen well. She elected to be born in London, the only daughter of an English mother and Greek father. The balance between extreme riches and the working class English roots of her mother had been achieved by skilled parenting. Her childhood holidays had found her running barefoot through the olive groves and learning to make goats cheese with women in a small Greek village where her father's family were well respected, living as they did, in the grand villa at the top of the hill. Another week would find her chatting to the neighbours in a small English terrace house in London's east end.

Her maternal grandmother had taught her to like and value everyone no matter what their background. She did not subscribe to the feeling of having roots and was happy just meeting people. Social class and materialistic values held little significance for her. Academic excellence was another matter. Both of her parents had encouraged her studies, nourishing the childhood thirst for knowledge that was so apparent in her early years. Her working class English mother had studied hard to move into the academic path of art and ancient philosophy. The maternal Greek research encouraged the young Lyre to willingly absorb knowledge and the natural beauty of the world.

Coming from parents who had not subscribed to their original strict Christian backgrounds also made her spiritual independence a valuable asset in this life. She had not been baptised into any religion, her third eye had neither been closed by the watery Christian cross on the end of an English vicar's finger or sealed with the holy oil of a Greek orthodox priest. No Chrism for her, no "sealing" of her energy centres. The anointing that was accompanied by the words "the seal of the gift of the Holy Spirit" from a well meaning priest was not her destiny. She would eventually have respect but not reverence for such ceremony. It could not have been a better gift of spiritual freedom for a young soul who was to become a wise and useful woman to guide many others through their lives.

As she grew up she preferred the real people from her childhood in both countries to the social climbers that she met at her father's cocktail parties in his London home. After falling in love with Lyre's mother he had migrated naturally to London to further the old family antiques and house design business. His own plush villa, demolished from mainland Greece shortly before his death, became his final project as it was rebuilt onto a beautiful island in the Cyclades. This private island was inhabited mostly by abandoned marble quarries when the family first established their summer retreat there and it eventually became a welcome quiet space for Lyre to meditate and recharge her batteries after busy, energy sucking seasons of work.

She had learned to value the ancient rocks and stones of her father's homeland, feeling the energetic vibrations deep within their mineral content. She loved the colours and structures of what she considered to be the naturally occurring toys of her childhood games. The multi faceted energies of this stone kingdom became her companions as she played under the hot sun beside the Aegean sea. She never felt lonely as she slipped into natural reveries, visualising soldiers from the crusades overthrowing the Byzantine Empire all around her. The scenarios that played out in front of her childish eyes were later corroborated in her English school history lessons. It was never a surprise to her that she had already seen the thirteenth century elegant Venetian Dukes or fierce looking sixteenth century Ottoman Turks and the Russian squadrons inhabiting the Greece of the seventeen hundreds.

Meditation came naturally to this peacefully serene child, although her family would have called it "day dreaming." They would sigh and smile and say, "What a dreamer our Lyre is, she'll need to get more focussed if ever she wants to make something of herself!" In spite of these childhood visions she professed to have not been born with a psychic gift. It was well known that she incorporated intuitive psychic and angel readings in her highly acclaimed consultations. She ran energy healing, medically intuitive workshops that helped many who had been dismissed by conventional drug based medicine. The use of predictive cards and meditation training and general lifestyle advice was profoundly valued by many who travelled to meet her from around London and the home-counties.

Her expertise and gifts were highly regarded for inspiring new thought processes in the rich and famous. The fact that she was not unduly impressed by the wealth or status of her clients, added to her appeal. By acknowledging that the problems of each client were built into their soul and not the outer trappings that society had afforded them she allowed a group consciousness to develop. The private clients came to her by word of mouth. Each time that she decided to cut back on her individual consultations another "friend of a friend" would be telephoning to seek help in her office or sometimes in another country where she held occasional surgeries. She was continually searching for other practitioners who worked in a similar credible way, seeking to spread the work and encourage other professionally qualified holistic therapists. When Georgina was born Lyre had sensed a new colleague would eventually cross her path. The inner knowing of soul energy groups were a great source of support to Lyre and her special friends. They always knew when a baby with certain gifts was returning to the earth plane. It was an exciting challenge to seek out that soul when it's earthly body grew to adulthood.

Dr Papakostas, as she was rarely called, took great satisfaction and comfort in her voluntary work. She often worked with those who had need of a spiritual lift or some kind of support for life's physical and mental traumas. Her favourite saying when she was just a young practitioner was "there but for the grace of God go I!" Thus she became well known for her non judgmental altruism although she never spoke of it herself.

Lyre socialised with an eclectic mix of people who worked in the spiritual/healing area or the arts. Her Greek antiquities and wine collections were a passion that she shared with those special friends. The Knightsbridge apartment had been adapted to provide a serene and tastefully decorated office space. The private rooms were decorated by a friend from her University days who was now a well known interior designer. Everything was designed to give a feeling of peace and wellbeing with pastel shades on furnishings complementing the cream backdrop. Occasionally a splash of exotic colour was provided by an artefact from her travels, an Indian prayer hanging or exquisitely carved screen that served to remind her of deeper meanings from other lives too.

She regularly cleaned the energy in her whole apartment to remove negative deposits from any client or friend who happened to have unburdened more than their words. It was well known that energies could be deposited in the atmosphere of a room or even within another person's aura. Many practitioners who shared her skills cleared their working space and homes to keep the electromagnetic field light and happy.

Sometimes a group of colleagues were called upon to do a collective clearing in friend's offices or homes if they had been inundated with a particularly heavy and unwelcome energy field. As the new lighter energies gathered in the Universe so the old and outdated tended to make a nuisance of themselves in the form of depressions, unexplained illnesses. These were the areas where Lyre and her colleagues were being increasingly called to help. She always kept an enormous pottery oil burner in her hall and office filling the air with essential oils of Frankincense, lavender, bergamot or lemon depending on the time or need. The large flat bottomed candles burned continuously inside the oven-like cave that allowed an integral bowl of oil and water mixed to sit comfortably on top as it diffused it's purifying and calming perfume to the atmosphere. Lyre's home and office was a very special space. Many people had commented upon the uniquely shaped oil burner when they visited. She had found it in Greece on one of her relaxing forays into the countryside. It had been produced by a local blind woman who worked the clay with love and passion before the individually designed pieces were fired with the original glazes that she could not see for herself. She often said she did not need to see because she could feel. She confided in Lyre that she only wished more people would "feel" their lives with their soul instead of just looking with their eyes.

Lyre loved interesting personalities and was easily enthused by characters for their charm and difference. She was well aware that she had occasionally been taken advantage of financially when traveling just because she had been mesmerised by someone's skill or gift that had intrigued her. Her English mother had often said "it takes all sorts" and she was happy to subscribe to this broad acceptance of mankind.

The obviously sophisticated taste in her choice of discrete designer clothes was offset by her hairstyle with the distinctive Cruella de Ville black and white dye to her smoothly topped quiff and an almost razor sharp back, adding length to her already long neck. The olive tinted complexion and dark oval eyes allowed her to get away with very little makeup, a drop of moisturiser and sweep of mascara to complete her daily routine. Her lips seemed to shine effortlessly without more than a quick brush of peach coloured gloss. The long shapely legs carried her slim body effortlessly without the need for gym workouts much to the disgust of several friends. What could have been an angular body shape was softened by large firm breasts, much admired but never to be touched by others in this lifetime.

She still loved her Greek goat's cheese and rich mimosa flavoured honey with black olives for breakfast each day. The local deli provided her favourite rough country style bread and conveniently also provided the freshly squeezed blood orange juice that she loved. The latest Nespresso machine nestling on her kitchen worktop had solved her coffee addiction for ever more. The fact that she liked to drive around in a beaten up old Volkswagen beetle (also black and white) gave a certain eclectic mix of style and earthiness that endeared her to many. Her intuition aided by many hours spent in deep meditation reminded her of her own previous lives, one of the more notable being as a Chinook Indian in the early eighteen hundreds.

As a newly graduated doctor in this life, she had travelled to the Pacific Northwest coast of America and had felt a familiar yearning as she sat by the Lower Columbia River. It was only later in meditation she saw herself as a tribal shaman. The meditative vision showed clearly that she was campaigning for the change in a tribal tradition. It had concerned her that high born Chinooks favoured flat heads for their children. This went to such an extent that babies' heads were flattened between planks of wood to produce the required skull shape. Although as a shaman herself she was considered to be of high rank she had campaigned to stop social discrimination in her own tribes. Evidently she had always been a social warrior for equality, no matter which century she was in. It was ironic that she was born into such a comfortable wealthy home this time, or perhaps it was her reward. Her karma was often discussed when she was with good friends who understood the field.

Another important part of that old life as a Chinook Shaman was the fur trader that she met and fell in love with. He eventually worked for the Hudson's Bay Company after starting his career in America as an explorer and fur trapper. He was a trail hardened, handsome, Frenchman with a no nonsense approach to life. He didn't suffer fools and had happily parted company with the original expedition leader who he had considered to be too weak to lead a group of explorers into the wild regions of the Northwest. They had met as she was roaming the forested area along the bay in her search for medicinal herbs. Her swarthy suntanned Beauty was not lost on him. She had taught him the Chinook language and he shared rudiments of French with her. The modern day Lyre discovered in her Google search, after this vision crept into her meditation, that the later development of the Chinook language has elements of French incorporated. She was thrilled to discover that Chinook longhouses had been discovered near the Oregon border, another place that felt familiar to her in this life. Such stored memories had been unsatisfactorily explained by naive scientists today as "traces of neurotransmitters in the brain influenced by cultural belief systems."

But Lyre knew otherwise. It was not surprising for her when she recognised the soul energy of great love from that past life in the Pacific North West. She had met the same energy in many other lifetimes as many different incarnations. That love energy had been initially physical, working from the power of lower chakras of her body but as the vibrational energy grew in each incarnation her kundalini power house allowed the higher chakras to activate and grow into spiritual love with all of the wonderful associated knowledge. The power and intensity of the electromagnetic field had developed with each reincarnation, as it gained knowledge, one of the other. But she had never had any doubts who it was this time.

Only this time there would be no physical love, the intensely sexual love and heart pounding physical yearning of the old lives was not to be needed again.

Chapter 7

Aramantha (Az)

The Porsche cayenne scrunched to a stop on the damp gravel drive in rural Buckinghamshire. Az rushed out of the house to greet her husband and daughter, her anxious face trying not to show her relief to have her daughter home safely.

"I told you that boy was bad news Isabelle thank goodness your dad was able to get there in time." "In time for what exactly mother?"

"They told me that drugs were going to be used and syringes would be exchanged without your knowing, you could have died or been infected with Aids."

"Oh Mum how could you possibly know that? There were only a few Es being passed around and I didn't touch them."

"I heard heroin and crack cocaine very clearly and you would not have even realised what was happening until it was too late."

At this point Karl, threw the car keys onto the hall table and stormed back into the drive, "For Christ's sake Az that's enough, Izzy is home safe and don't start that barmy stuff about hearing voices."

"But I was told Izzy was in danger and look how you were able to help her, so that can't be mad can it?"

"Mother's intuition is one thing but voices, from god knows where, are another and I don't want to hear any more about it. I'm pouring a glass of wine if you want one, or shall I call that new psychiatrist in town?"

Aramantha stopped speaking and resigned herself to being regarded as some kind of freak in her own home once more. She looked towards her husband and daughter as they exchanged knowing glances and realised that she had been sharing too much of her information again. Until recent years she had managed to accept and use her cosmic energy channelling in a discrete way. When she and Karl had first got together he had labelled her as "quirky and cute" She always seemed to be able to recognise something was about to happen before anyone else. He had been, she thought, a little proud of her back then. He had loved her cuddly curves and bouncy auburn curls and often squeezed her affectionately as they wandered the Scottish streets of her home town before they were married.

Karl and Aramantha had been students at the London School of Economics before he ended up in Accountancy and Financial management. She went into teaching where her degree in English and ancient history was well used. Her classes had been welcomed as students responded well to her apple cheeks, button nose and glowing skin, burnished by the sea air from her native Dundee. Growing up in Scotland's fourth largest city on the banks of the Firth of Tay had afforded her time to sense the medieval roots of this city. Her soul could remember when it had been a Scottish burgh before it's rapid expansion into the city of "jute, jam and journalism" during the nineteenth century. Her present incarnation enjoyed its famous Dundee cake and fruity, rind filled marmalade. Her voluptuous curves bore witness to this preference for all things sweet. The students were inspired by her inherent knowledge of ancient times, remembering as she did, her old lives without the text books.

The London life had moved Aramantha away from her Scottish "seer" Mum with a reputation of being "fey" by the neighbours. The marriage to Karl had seemed like a perfect match sharing their young idealistic vision of improving the world through better management and broad ranging education. He had not been overly concerned about her daily meditation and yoga sessions. Indeed he just called her "spooky Az" without stopping to consider why or how it worked to keep her sane in the city rat race.

When Isabelle had arrived they had moved to the countryside, following the tradition of Karl's "something in the city" colleagues. Aramantha had honed her enthusiasm for the other dimensions into watching her baby daughter cooing and waving to the spirit friends who came to visit her on a daily basis. The fact that Az, too, could see and communicate with these misty souls gave mother and daughter a secret bond that there never seemed to be a reason to share with a third party, let alone hard working Karl who zoomed off to London each day to provide for his family.

"Look mummy, that lady in our garden is wearing a lovely dress right down to the floor, and she is waving at me."

"Yes darling, she is happy that you can see her, she lived in this house a long time ago and likes knowing that there is a pretty little girl living here now."

Inevitably, as the baby grew into a little girl and became more involved with the concrete world of school friends and books she became less connected to the other dimensions and her ability to see spiritual energy just disappeared. As with most children by the time she was five or six she had completely forgotten those hazy friends who had shared happy summer afternoons in the garden with her cuddly relaxed Mum.

Az, too, had re-focused as she became preoccupied with bringing up her daughter, attending school functions, baking for local fundraisers and popping up to London to shop and meet old friends for lunch. She limited her meditation time to the odd hour when she knew that the house was empty and the family tasks were completed. Once a month she and Karl would spend a Friday evening in the city and take in a show or dinner whilst kindly Mrs Barnes from the village babysat. She had realised that in recent years it was only with her old friend, Lyre, that she could feel really free and just be herself. They met rarely whilst Isabelle was in primary school. As the girl grew into her teens and needed less mothering Az was able to meet Lyre more regularly either in London, where they visited esoteric bookshops before lunching or attended Mind Body Spirit exhibitions together. When Lyre flew off to do weekend workshops around Europe and the States she had often invited Aramantha to go along. She never went, of course, because Karl would just not understand.

Az could not tell her husband when she met Lyre and would not even consider telling him about her visits to esoteric shops. Books on spiritual or new age topics were smuggled into her small study beside the kitchen. As Karl had aged and become more involved in the very concrete world of banking, hedge funds and investors he made it clear that he considered her less "quirky" and more "mad." Their marriage consequently matured into a dull, predictable, sex on Sundays, virtually uncommunicative partnership. They lived parallel lives within the same home, occasionally coming together to continue to function as a family unit. He brought home the funds and she ran the home, taking total responsibility for all three of them. Somewhere along the line they had acquired a beautiful, ivy covered, home in the countryside, large garden with weekly gardener, cleaner and an assortment of family pets. The statutory chocolate coloured Labrador accompanied her green wellied legs to the local village shops as she selected fresh organic produce for the highly praised family meals. She had learned to conform to the social norms quite well given her unconventional background and previously well "tuned in" status. The only small rebellion she made until now was her choice of car. She refused to conform to the four by four brigade and indulged herself with a burgundy MG midget. She knew that her daughter enjoyed being driven to school, hair flying in even the coolest of English weather, with the lid off her little car. She noticed that Izzy too called it a "lid off car" rather than a sports car or more sedate sounding cabriolet.

The night of Izzy's rescue from the very dodgy party was the beginning of a new phase in all of their lives. Karl seemed to make a decision from that time on to sort her out. She heard him using these words to his mother on the phone. Her mother in law lived in Cumbria, far enough away to need to be invited for planned visits and yet close enough to travel to them by train without too much fuss. It had been their shared northern roots (Scotland and Cumbria being mutually supportive in their suspicion of London life) that had been an initial attraction at the LSE. There was much less sharing of anything these days she thought. He was using his exasperated voice as he confided in his mother.

"I'll have to do something to get her sorted out, it is becoming an embarrassment to us both Mum. Yes Izzy is quite upset by the references to alternative medicine, clairvoyants and now these bloody voices she says she hears." Karl looked over his shoulder to check that he was not being overheard. "Yes, you do? That's great, could you organise an appointment for her? I'll suggest it for her next trip to London. We could make it a day out in disguise I think."

Az walked away from this patronising and yet expected conversation. What had her wonderfully exciting Mother always said, "eavesdroppers never hear good of themselves"? That certainly seemed to be correct right then. She could feel panic and frustration welling up inside her and tried to centre herself to decide how she should deal with this development. She had neglected her personal meditation time for many years now, not wanting to be interrupted when she was away in the cosmic energies that she had once found so comforting. She decided this was the time to seek some personal guidance for herself, at long last. She called into the lounge that she was off to walk the dog and that their dinner was in the oven. She could sense father and daughter shrugging to themselves. They would decide that she was once more exhibiting menopausal stress as she strode purposefully out of the front door.

Why was she feeling so unable to stand up for herself in this lifetime? She often asked the sky what was the lesson this time around. She fully acknowledged that she was a spiritual energy on a life lesson in the earth body that she had been born into. Her mother had been a big influence in her life. Together they had been able to discuss many topics that would have shocked Karl and his conservative, middle class mother. Az's well educated mother had been born into a simple family of Scottish farm labourers. The understanding of nature that she shared with her daughter had evolved naturally from the long country walks so coveted by mother and daughter. Their topics ranged from herbal medicine to politics and ancient history that they both loved. They knew that they had met in other lives, well remembered from ancient times. Both mother and daughter accepted that their roles had often been exchanged and they could advise and counsel each other accordingly. Together they would watch the young Isabelle play in the large country garden as she acknowledged her spirit friends and even the odd angel came to visit. They had marvelled together as an enormous angelic energy field came to visit the bedside of a very sick 2 year old Izzy. "Wow, mummy, bootiful angel holding Izzy's hand, fank you."

Yes, she missed her mother every day that she had been gone. Perhaps it was time to enlist the support and wisdom of her old friends on a more professional basis before she was wheeled into the psychiatrists office by her well meaning, but spiritually dead, mother in law.

Az walked towards the wooded heath-land behind the house, her emotions in turmoil, but with renewed determination to change this pattern of arguments, scathing comments and her own withdrawal from family life to protect the marriage that seemed to be fast approaching a rocky shore. The spring evening was cool and breezy as she stomped across the slightly damp grass. The chocolate lab skipped happily along beside her, oblivious to her angry and confused state. How she yearned for her mother's guidance and kindly voice right now. Her sudden death just a few years ago had been a great loss to many. Az and her daughter, Izzy, had felt quite bereft for a very long time. Her waxed jacket suddenly started to vibrate and she stopped still, wondering if she was getting a download from her mother's spirit. It made her laugh to herself when she realised that she had left her cell phone in her pocket, on silent mode, since a recent shopping trip. As she flipped the opening she saw that it was Lyre, as if by divine guidance, ringing for a chat. She sank gratefully to sit on the bottom bar of a country style that bridged a pedestrian path between fields on the heath. The view from here was pretty rolling countryside and somewhere that she often rested on her walks with the dog. In happier years she had sat in just that spot, with a baby Isabelle on her knee watching her husband and dog running around the green fields to entertain the giggling toddler.

"Oh Lyre you have no idea how happy I am to hear from you right now. Or perhaps you do?"

"Well my dear girl, something, somewhere told me that perhaps you could do with a chat, in fact I'm not sure, but it may have been your mother."

"Could well have been, as I was just thinking of her a minute ago. I really do miss her." Aramantha tried not to allow the brimming tears brimming to flow over. When she heard the kindness from her old friend she could feel the floodgates of combined relief and sadness starting to open. She held it together when she felt the need to defend or protect herself at home but when she could relax and be herself it was not so easy.

"It's ok you know." Lyre sympathised gently. "You can let it out."

"What? Oh yes I know Lyre, I have forgotten how to just BE, you know to be in this moment and be me I suppose."

Lyre was smiling on the other end of the line, "That's why I was saying just let go because we know it will be alright when it should be, if you get my drift?"

"It's just that I really do need to remember that I have a gift too, like Mum had and I know I should acknowledge it, much more than I have done in the last few years. It is so easy to get bogged down in the practicalities of this world and let my left brain control rather than allow myself to be spiritually influenced."

"Wouldn't worry about that Az most of us are the same, it's just that I have been given a bigger remit this time around and I know that is why I have chosen to remain single and celibate for my sins! Sometimes a bit of mattress shaking wouldn't go amiss." A throaty chuckle echoed down the line as both Lyre and Az remembered previous lives with more sexual action around. "There is a big job to do before the shift from 2012 into 2013 changes the vibrations once more. How are you anyway?"

By the time Az had finished relating the whole explosive tale she was starting to feel the effects of the damp wooden style on her ample backside. As she eased herself up, much to the bored dogs delight, Lyre was already processing the situation in her own unique way.

"It seems like you're ready for rebalancing your life path before you get stuck on a camino not initially of your choice. We both know that once we are stuck, then fear has taken over. It's alright to be cautious, that's natural before change happens but we don't want fear to take hold to prevent any natural movement in a forward and improved direction. So you have to take back your power right now or as soon as possible?"

"You're right there, I have been so busy tiptoeing around the family (and the mother in law) for ruddy years now, that I had almost forgotten who I was." Aramantha took a breath to suppress what could have been a sob as she pulled a paper tissue from her pocket. "Oh, I know they love me as much as I love them (at least I hope so) but our differences have become so obvious if I don't just conform and keep quiet about the old inner wisdom. To be honest, I gave up bothering so as not to start a row. I almost feel surplus to requirements in the family at the moment." She stood up to chase a plastic dog's poo bag that had tumbled from her pocket with the paper tissue and was blowing away in the light breeze that came across the heath. She was listening to Lyre as she puffed along to snare the empty bag.

"At least you haven't forgotten the power of heart energy. If we forget the power of the heart's message then we are on the way down that slippery plug hole to depression and unnecessary anxiety. How many clients do I meet who have just given up on their own happiness because they have forgotten, if indeed they ever knew, their life mission and the bigger picture that is on its way. I get so frustrated with the silly gits that sometimes I just want to shake them. Now I know I'm getting old. Where is all that love and light stuff I used to feel?"

"You can say that again. Remember Eilish, who used to say send them love and light and fuck 'em? Well she was so right. Got it!" Aramantha had put her foot onto the bag at last and stuffed it into her pocket with a feeling of having at least achieved something useful today. "Lord, sorry, Lyre, I was just chasing a poo bag while we chatted, how times have changed when it gave me such satisfaction to get hold of it. Sad or what?"

"Little pleases the innocent as they say. Anyway I've been spouting off about all the things that you know What we need is a plan of action for you right now. You say that a psychiatric assessment is imminent?"

Lyre then spoke at length about her ideas, all the time subconsciously sending visualisations to Aramantha's receptive mind. The idea of a psychiatric intervention was both disturbing and scary. Az walked and listened as she absorbed so many things in a multi sensory way that she felt quite exhilarated for the first time in some weeks. The two friends hatched a plan to deal with Aramantha's family and the psychiatrist.

Suddenly it was less threatening and more fun. She could smell the damp grass as it stuck to her shoes, the Hawthorne blossom in the hedgerows and the richer aroma of cow dung from the local farms. The skylarks were singing over head in the still light sky and early bees were starting to buzz over the dandelions bowing their golden heads with dampness form the earlier rain. She took deep breaths as she listened to her friend's wise words, her limbs were moving smoothly like the legs of a much younger and slimmer woman. She was transported back to those days when her young family romped around this heath land without a care in the world. Her only regret was that she had not held firm to her ancient knowledge and continued to discuss those spirit energies that she knew her daughter had seen as a baby and toddler. How easily did societal norms slip onto her shoulders?

Boat rocking was hard work; it had been much easier to just jump in the same boat as the rest of her family and friends. So many of the local women, living similar life styles to her were very conservative indeed, nodding quietly when they agreed with a conversation and just bringing a polite hand to their chests when they "couldn't possibly agree" and silently patting themselves to keep quiet rather than argue a point, any point at all. She called the accompanying expressions on these occasions the "sucked lemon faces." How she wished that some of them would raise their voices and express their feelings more honestly. Conforming to a quiet English lady life was so easy but it could be repressively soul destroying for her once spiritual soul. Lyre's skill in sensory downloading had allowed her to not only see, but also feel the joy and love of what had been, so recently, and what she now knew could be, again.

It was going to take some work on Aramantha's part and very careful handling but she knew she could do it. In fact she knew that she had no choice. She, too, was starting to remember why she was here.

Chapter 8

Eoin and Georgina

Eoin was nestled cosily into the bell tower of St Martin-in-the-Fields in London. The statue of Lord Nelson often appeared to wink at him across Trafalgar square, if he looked closely enough. Now that pigeons were banned from the ancient square Nelson looked much more ship shape and clean. More accurately the feeding of pigeons had been banned, consequently you could now walk there without worrying about what was stuck to your shoes. Not that Eoin needed to walk there at all in his present role. He remembered his old pal Nelson from other lives, of course. Eoin had memories of the battle of Trafalgar when he had been a ship's boy, the smell of tarry ropes still evoked memories of the rough seas off Cadiz. He liked this particular vantage point, overlooking Trafalgar Square because he had once been buried deep below the old foundations of the present church, in the year 413 when it really was "in the fields". In yet another medieval life, before randy King Henry the eighth rebuilt the church, he had roamed the cloisters as a monk. This was in between the lives where he had known Lyre, Aramantha and Georgina in different roles and relationships back in the ancient Pyrenees. He could remember lives of varying lengths and debatable learning experiences, where he had roamed the world as a Tibetan Buddhist, French philosopher, fur trader of course and Italian police woman amongst many other reincarnations too numerous to recount. He felt that he had earned his present energy form. His role as a spirit

60

guide and general energetic presence was to support earthbound souls during and after their lives embodied on the planet earth.

The junior angel, Ramese, was once more seconded to Eoin's care as Archangel Jophiel was working in three different countries today, simultaneously spreading love and light to some war zones. Ramese enjoyed the knowledge that was imparted by the almost incessant chat, regurgitated from Eoin's inner depths.

"Just think how the human DNA is evolving to such an extent that cognitive mechanisms are about to lose the ability to process innovative thought. The lemmings and the sheep can easily be lead by anyone with an authoritative voice. I wonder who the next weird guru will be, you know the ones who stick on an Indian necklace, headbands and some baggy trousers and start sending photos out on the net where they try to look beatific to gather needy followers around them. Even Jesus himself laughs at the lookalikes who want to start a new cult." He managed to look wryly amused at his own words whilst the beautifully feathered angel hovered around the clocks on the outside of the tower listened intently to Eoin.

"You know Ramese, I really must have a word with a higher power to ask why pre programming, so carefully selected before re incarnation, is still being instantly forgotten within years or even months of a baby being born with its newly allocated soul." Eoin appeared to drift around the bell tower as he thought out his words of wisdom for the express purpose of this morning's role as mentor to apprentice angels. "It seems about time now with higher vibrations in the Universe that we allow kids to keep their memories that are present at birth, rather than letting them lose all that inner, hard earned, wisdom to start all over again in this life.

What a waste! No wonder we have so many sad souls drugging themselves to death before their agreed time!" Ramese nodded so enthusiastically at this that the clock face in front of him moved it's big hand by 5 minutes in the airflow. Even the few renegade pigeons in the square lifted off in a flock of surprised grey feathers. "Look at that, seems nobody told the pigeons that they're not welcome any more. Used to be so much fun watching tourists removing poo from their hats!"

Ramese giggled in a high pitched way, to cover his embarrassment that he had, in a manner of speaking, moved time.

"Well must go, thanks for the chat young man, although I know you're androgynous and could be young woman or whatever you chose, for all I know." At this Eoin floated his vibrational molecular field out of the bell tower and drifted off towards the Camden Road to one of University College London's Hall's of residence. The very white, newly feathered, young angel, replaced Eoin's energy field in the bell tower and smiled bemusedly as he subtly readjusted the big hand on the clock face. He so hoped that this movement in time had been not been noticed by any of the bustling crowds below. He heard Eoin's words from afar

"Say hello to Jophiel and wish him well with his peacemaking."

When Eoin met Georgina she was just about ready to tell the earthbound world how it was in the greater Universe. She had reached the magic age of thirty three when it is personal crucifixion or survival time. It had been hard for her getting to that age relatively un scarred for a "seer." He thought this an apt term for those who stay connected with the other dimensions after their birth into the physical world. He really did wish that he had been allowed to remember so much the last time around. He was here to explain the detail of that soul connection to previous lives for her final thesis. This was to be a thesis that would cause quite a ripple in academic and esoteric circles for several years to come. He felt sure of it.

She was scratching her head in the "grounding" chapter of her thesis, as the laptop would not type the words that she sought. Until that time she had found all of the extra concepts that she needed in various philosophical, religious and pseudo religious texts from the internet and libraries. Her research trips to centres of excellence in America and Japan had given her a surfeit of information. She had marvelled at just how similar the so called diverse religious beliefs were. The most important concepts, that were often verified in religious texts, seemed to have downloaded directly into her mind, during meditation or even whilst typing, almost like a computer download. In fact she had learned to trust her own instincts as the words seemed to pour onto the page as though she were a funnel or one of those plastic conduits that she had watched her dad install into the new kitchen walls to feed the electrical cables through.

Yes, a conduit, she thought. She liked that analogy very much indeed.

Right about now she was hearing the word "connected" but was not getting the explanations that she needed to discuss the soul on its early journey on earth. The captain's office chair that had been a present from her family was turning on it's pedestal as she executed the swivel that always helped her to think. She loved the deep buttoned, green leather seat for it its comfort over the long study hours that her PhD had needed. It was her one concession to comfort and out of style with the rest of the meagrely furnished tiny study, come dormitory that she now occupied. Her hands went up to her scalp and lifted her silky long hair from the roots as she swivelled the chair in her thinking mode. She was not prepared for the powerful energy field sitting on her bed.

She dropped her hands with shock and just stared at the rapidly solidifying figure that was Eoin. He was glowing from the top of his silver grey head to the bottom of his navy blue deck shoes. Today's outfit with collarless shirt was open at the neck in the style of the hippy generation, luckily he was not wearing beads or shoulder length hair or she would have been more incredulous than she already was. He looked like a well groomed professional guy on his way to his boat at the weekend. Except, of course, that there was a really glowing aura all around him. It appeared as though a light were being carefully shone from behind to cast him in holographic silhouette. Georgina was by now well used to apparitions of passed over spiritual energy asking for her help. This was different.

Here was a kindly and quite stylish, granddad, glowing with what she realised was loving energy, offering to help in response to her thoughts. Not only that, he arrived gently without fuss and, as was his habit, already speaking.

"Some souls are re allocated with a small degree of choice into earth bound bodies at the moment of birth. There are some who are allocated to a body and new life whilst they are still in the womb to give them time to adjust to their new earth mother and new prospective family. Ah yes, those are the poor wee buggers subjected to baby Beethoven music, gentle massage through the engorged stomach or the hypnotherapy tapes of the pregnant Mum. Such pre natal experiences are infinitely better than those who hear the fights and bickering, of course. Those uterine walls are never thick enough to save the torment of a reincarnated soul trying to settle in as it were, without too much disturbance."

Here he paused for breath, to smile at her, although she was certain that he was not actually breathing through the all encompassing glow, now filling her room. She started to rise from her favourite chair, but felt his energy pushing her gently back down.

"Sorry to burst in like this my dear!" He flapped his hand at her in a conciliatory manner that did not seem to fit with his unearthly glow.

"Most modern trends have been for the soul's energetic umbilical link to be 95% severed at birth at the same time as the physical cord is cut. Severed, that is, from the greater Universal consciousness until they can deal with the ancient wisdom in their new bodies. The problem has been that earth bodies have never been very good at coping with their ancient knowledge until the final stretch, sometimes not until months or even days before their recall to base. So, that has kind of messed up the greater plan for saving the planet. It's always romantic and enigmatic, of course, to hear of souls "seeing the light" just before the lights go out for them on earth. I mean what's that all about? What were they DOING down here and why did they think they had been given a return ticket in the first place?"

The gushing almost camp tone of these rhetorical questions made her giggle to herself without any fear and with an underlying surety that she had seen this person before. He had levitated slightly as he became quite passionate during the last pronouncement. Georgina found herself engrossed watching his energy field as it pulsated with light whilst rising slowly, although still in the sitting position.

"You do know Georgina how lucky you have been to remain relatively unscathed by this human society that has been nurturing you for over thirty years now don't you?"

This pertained to the fact that she had not been declared schizophrenic or found to be suffering from grand mal epilepsy as had happened to a few of the friends from her various psychic development groups.

"Nor have you been given that vulgar and meaningless label of "mad" but have actually been allowed the dignity of Benin "different" without too much fuss amongst family and friends. A few centuries earlier and you may well have been burned as a witch or suspicious medicine woman, Oh, I forgot, that already happened to you in 1502 and 1600, sorry dear. Just imagine a few years earlier you could've been Jeanne d'Arc, lucky you missed that dubious honour." He used the French pronunciation for Joan of Arc as he flapped his hand at her again to show his empathy.

"Oh yes I know that now, but, well hello anyway, err Mr ..?"

"Just call me Eoin, we have met in other lives, but you won't remember me yet, it'll come … … Oh my dear, it would have been so easy for you to join the tea leaf readers and fairground kiosk brigade of Gypsy Rose Lees who seem to survive by dispensing the odd pearl of ancient wisdom amongst a whole lot of waffle." She put up her hand to interrupt him.

"That's true, yes, but I have been subject to the usual distrust and petty jealousy because I am different. My generic label of "weird Georgina" has usually helped the cynics to dismiss any value I may have had whenever I stepped outside the box to help someone having difficulties. But you probably know this as you obviously know me?" She sighed with the inevitability of it all.

"Oh I know that not all of those people are quacks just as some are ethical and conscientious as you know. But things are changing. I have a good friend who spends a lot of her life teaching people how to use their intuition in such matters. Yo know what I mean, a feeling in your gut about who is credible and who isn't? But that's another story."

Georgina was now standing to put the kettle on before she realised, with a slight blush to her cheeks, that her visitor would most certainly not be able to take tea with her.

"We are well aware, Georgina, that your psychological and professional survival came about as a result of your quest for knowledge. You knew that from your first day on earth, you needed to know a lot of things quickly. Thanks to Thomas, also, I have to say, you devoured books about folk lore, the modern sciences, philosophy and theology from an early age. There was never any doubt about your need to communicate from that first day. It was even obvious to your loving family as your wise little eyes went beyond the expression that caused all the grannies to say - Oh, that one's been here before – she is definitely an old soul!"

She wanted to ask how he knew Thomas, because it seemed odd that he had never mentioned this obviously special person. But she had other things to corroborate.

"I once surprised my Mam by telling her that I knew she had cried for a whole day after my long birth, even though I had been put into an incubator for a few hours to help me accept this world. I don't think that I was too keen to stay at first, almost like I knew there was a big job ahead. I so felt Mam's fear that I may not live and my little soul tried to comfort her, in fact I am sure that is why I stayed as she was so frightened that I would die in the first day."

He was nodding sympathetically, acknowledging that so many new babies have to accept their new bodies in each reincarnation. Some just don't want to stay to complete their life mission and some have already done their job in a short time just by being held in their grieving parents' arms.

"Yes, it is wonderful when new parents who, unfortunately, lose their babies, close to birth, learn that the little soul came to give them something in even just a few hours on this earth. Holding a precious little body for a short time often gives great wisdom and comfort to parents when they get time to come to terms with the loss, they can also see what they gained too."

"Love!" they both said together and then laughed in unison as though they had always known each other. "Ngariad i, how lucky I was to have so much love in my childhood from day one really, Mam used to look at me with such shining love from her eyes 'mabi fi..' she would say … 'f'anwylyd' I so remember, my baby, my beloved, so old fashioned now to hear this in Welsh, but I felt so cherished."

This visit from Eoin, although he had not paused long enough to tell her his previous names, was the climax of her life so far. She really was itching to get a soft lead pencil in her hands to sketch this vision of light and wisdom nestled on her bed right now. Her artistic ability had often been remarked upon too. The famous visit by 6 year old Georgie to the London Science Museum had moved into family legend. She sketched for the whole homeward journey as the high speed train transported her and the indulgent gran to their small Welsh town. When she grew tired of the drawing she resorted to her other favourite pass time of giving gran a mesmeric head massage. Gran was delighted and surprised to see a perfectly reproduced façade of the Cromwell Road Science Museum springing in almost three D perfection from the page. She would not be surprised to learn that Eoin had been gazing over their shoulders wishing that he could have a chat with them about it, right there and then. Over twenty five years later his time had now come. It had been somewhat irritating for him when he knew that he had the answers to many of those rhetorical questions that she had made to the atmosphere where he happened to be floating around on so many other occasions in the past. He went on to explain his personal frustrations at not being allowed to make himself known to her before.

"I did so want to speak to you, many times, especially when you were having teenage problems with morons who were jealous of your serenity. Some hard lessons we just have to learn for ourselves you know? It is not only with you that I have felt these frustrations, it is a general problem I have with responding to orders from above, so to speak. Free will is a very big part of being human you know?"

Georgina was swinging round in her chair yet again as she turned to consult her laptop. "You know that is the thing when academic researchers are looking at psychic phenomena, I heard it in many of those centres when they were wondering why someone has chosen to ignore or not comment on psychically received information." She was running her finger down the screen to see where she had noted this in her reports. He was quick to jump in as she moved her concentration to the file names on screen.

"OK so, I admit that I have made the usual bangs on the furniture and puffs of air in front of faces. I have been particularly skilled at making TV and computer screens go "ping" when they are not connected to the electricity. I even help books to fall from shelves, mirrors to drop, all the stuff from the sci-fi movies. The fact remains that there are none so blind as those who will not see, or I should say "feel" I suppose. It is essential that the human body recognises those feelings associated with an energy force around them. The old ladies used to say "ooh someone's just walked over my grave," when I wafted past them. They knew that they felt something but because of the societal conditioning at the time they associated the sensation with death and graves, not so far wrong when I come to think of it."

Here he stopped for a deep throated laugh and seemed quite pleased with his own thoughts. She turned from the screen having highlighted a document that she wanted to discuss with this gift from the Universe. But once more he was up and running with the theme.

"I would like them to have alluded to something less frightening and more positive of course. I think my energy and that from my pals in the angelic realms is very positive and could be so useful in the earth life if it was just recognised and acknowledged. I have to say that the angelic realms are a much higher vibration than my own humble levels although we do some pretty good co-operative work when the need arises." He appeared to snuggle down onto the pretty flowered duvet although he could not possibly bring any real weight onto the bed. Georgina was sure that she saw the duvet make a slight indent as he settled once more.

"So, now, where were we?" Eoin seemed to remember that he was here to answer her questions that would facilitate the final thesis write up.

"Well I was asking about how best to explain the term 'connected' as a concept that allows us to know that we all have some kind of spiritual connection to other dimensions and other people. I think that you have already helped me immensely, I just wonder why I have never seen or sensed your presence before."

At this point Eoin appeared to puff up his chest in preparation for another speech.

"If we think more about what society likes to think of as mechanistic thought processes being lost if we do not use them then I think it is not surprising. Although you are using much more than mechanical, concrete brain power here you are using that elusive sixth sense that centuries of philosophers and scientists have tried to deny. Add to this the fact that Science has continually harped on that if we cannot see or touch something we cannot measure it "empirically" and therefore it does not exist! Then you will have most certainly been influenced by the status quo whether you believed in other energies or not." He stopped to gaze about her room as if checking that there was no offensive, brain washing literature hanging on the wall.

"If the world continues to take "science" as its new God we will narrow our horizons even more than the flat earth bods although I reckon that football is fast becoming the new religion anyway and many cannot see past a goal post." He stood up to mime a goal scoring action energy sparks flying from his elegantly shoed foot. She giggled in spite of her interest and nodded supportively.

"If we are not allowed to acknowledge anything that is not seen and measurable then we will become increasingly boring and fearful of change. You know what I mean ? Science is being blocked by centuries old assumptions that have become dogmas. Step outside that narrow, so called scientific, box and you are dead. Come to think of it being dead is much more interesting when you are allowed to expand your consciousness from the ultimate unconsciousness so to speak. I would recommend doing the expanding of consciousness from the subconscious though whilst still in a living body. That way you get to remember what you find once you dig it out of that unused area of individual ability. Consciousness is much more than brain activity, physics and chemistry have been unable to prove anything more than mechanistic medical dogma. Thank goodness some new schools of science are beginning to dare to study stored memories as more than a random accumulation of neurotransmitters."

Georgina started to shuffle in her chair as she really did need that cup of tea about now to cope with the influx of words from this still glowing presence. She interjected;

"Yes but they have to be very brave, going against the mainstream and as you say years of dogma that has viewed us as machines with no soul at all. Or worse still a God, as an old long bearded guy who is some kind of engine driver who pushes our buttons without considering our own free will!"

Eoin smiled broadly as his energy field buzzed with little sparks;

"I can see that I'm not losing you here. It is not at all complicated if only we can find a way to explain in lay man's language. Go on get yourself that cuppa whilst I waffle on. I do know that a lot of earth based fear stops a lot of development."

She nodded and said "yes the fear of the fear, I have seen it so often." She wandered towards the kettle as spoke. Eoin continued with enthusiasm.

"Tell me about it. I know that several of my own passing overs would have been so much easier and more readily accepted and understood had I had more time to work with my deeper soul whilst I was truly alive. Don't get me wrong I am not advocating death before your time, just the opposite in fact. I am advocating learning about death and the soul whilst you are functioning in a living body as a means to better enjoy and fully experience your earth life. I see so many soul stuck in their bodies that do not work too well as a result of their minds not working well. This 'mind, body, soul' stuff didn't come from nowhere did it? The hedonistic life is ok if it is balanced into a meaningful contribution to society wherever that may be."

He shuffled about once more as his aura expanded to hit all four walls of the room, to such an extent that Georgie could feel warm tingles all over her body as she found the tea bags to make herself a cup of earl grey.

"Wherever your soul chose to incarnate is wherever you are supposed to start your life journey but it does not mean you have to stay there, oh no, the world is your oyster, it really is. I mean look at you, small town girl moves to London to study then travels to other countries to do the research. You could end up anywhere at all in this big world. Nothing is set in stone. The nuclear family of parents and two point something children, living up the road from where the parents were born is long gone."

Georgina needed to add her own ideas here. "Small *village* girl actually, but yes I know what you mean. My problem is that I'm happy to live wherever I am at any one moment in time. Roots don't seem to matter to me, don't tell my Mam that as she really does think I will be back to live around the corner when I have finished my studies." She poured the hot water on to the tea bag in her Portmeirion pottery mug that her mother had sent for fond memories of home. "Although I do sometimes wonder why I was born where I was, even with the understanding that it was my own pre birth choice."

"Ah! easy one that dear girl, you needed a loving, supportive beginning with just a bit of spice added by the brothers to help you stand up for yourself. No good coming into this work that you have chosen if you don't understand love and confidence. One normally leads to the other but not necessarily. I've seen many flunk their life mission because they just couldn't stand up for their inherent beliefs."

She was nodding again, whilst sipping her tea. "I always felt lots of love around me no doubt about that. I am so grateful to have had a loving family, good friends too. And you're right the teasing from two elder brothers was good training for lots more ribbing at university when I was out of my comfort zone where no one knew me."

"Good choice, Georgina dear, although maybe you could have had a soupçon more physical hard work in the early years to toughen up that delicate little body of yours!"

"I know what you mean. Hill walking was my limit at home but I have started going to the gym here in London though. It was a good way of broadening my friendship circle and getting away from this narrow academic bunch who hang out in the student's union. The gym nights do often end up in the local wine bar or at my girl friend Kyrie's, so not sure it so useful." She chuckled to herself as Eoin shook his head with a knowing smile.

"Oh all that "my body is my temple" stuff has its place but let's not get too carried away with self adulation or deprivation. Balance in all things I say. Masochistic, self flagellation was supposed to have disappeared from the earth in the medieval era. I enjoyed most of my lives, no matter what colour my skin, whether I was fat, thin, male or female, the body just wasn't important once I got to know my soul energy, but what a blessed long time it took. Of course many things were also supposed to have passed away from everyday life by now, like misogyny and homophobia but somewhere along the line some needy souls forgot that we all came from the same genetic code millions of years ago, and they screwed up their life mission and the preferred pattern of sociological evolution. Luckily, new energies are emerging now in different soul groups."

If new energies are supposed to arrive with each new generation then Georgina was a good illustration of such energy. Her artistic ability has already been mentioned but her childhood of modelling lumps of plasticine into amazingly accurate caricatures of friends and family was equalled in skill by the beach sandcastles resembling Egyptian tombs. When the other childish castle builders were struggling with emptying the little plastic buckets in one up turn she was already working turrets and tombs with her tiny fingers into places she had not yet seen in this life. As she thought about this she could swear that her thoughts were being projected onto the wall of her room, yes there were the sandcastles and her small self on holidays in Rhyll.

Eoin was nodding warmly towards the projected images that she realised they could both see. It felt like two old people watching a TV programme as they chatted. *Now* it was getting bizarre even for her open mind.

"You must know, by now my child, that you are a good example of an earth based spiritual energy who also has a body and wisdom crafted and very quickly remembered from previous lives. You *are* remembering very quickly now aren't you?"

She shook her head to clear the image on the wall from her mind.

"I certainly have started to remember much more whilst researching and writing this thesis. I always knew that there were the other dimensions to recognise because of seeing spirit since I was a small child. I am lucky that I learned pretty early in life that I need not be afraid when I could see an energy that wanted to talk to someone who was on earth. I suppose that I have met a weird mix of earthbound and stratosphere floating souls. Some became more significant than others. I like to think that I have helped some sad and grieving people by passing messages after loss, sometimes I wondered if I was doing the right thing."

"Oh you were my dear, you were, believe me."

"Listening to you now I can believe that some of those spirits were from the angelic realms and perhaps even higher in the scheme of Universal dimensions."

He nodded enthusiastically. and said …

"I must tell you that everything that we encounter on this earth is there to become our teacher for better or worse. Every single encounter or situation will make their mark on our soul as well as our bodies. Some of the vibrational energy collected into our aura, from other people and situations, well, we really do *not* need most of that old shit," Here he coughed to show that he knew that he had used a lower value word. "and this *stuff* has to be removed from our energy field or given back to where it belonged or our ultimate passing over will be more like a drowning than a floating off." With these words Eoin had started to float in the air once more.

"Come to think of it this actually seems to be a pretty good description of the end of life on earth – to drown or to float up – Mmm! .... To drown or not to drown that is the question."

Georgina decided that she really needed another mug of tea as she watched his energy disappear somewhere near the curtain pole.

Chapter 9

The Friends

The main street door was lying open as Georgina arrived to visit Kyrie. The entrance hall to the modern apartments was sparse and clean but lacked the character that Georgina hoped to find in her next home. The outlook from the front door was of more redbrick newly built apartment blocks. It had been quite a trek from her UCL student halls on the Camden Road to this smart new home recently occupied by Kyrie and Georgina's old friend Bronwen from her Welsh home village. They had chosen Tooting, south of the river and near to a park as the base for their first flat sharing venture. She was secretly pleased that she had helped to forge this new friendship between the girls who were her best friends. It had led to their signing a rental contract together in this bright new two bed-roomed living space. Kyrie was now working in St George's hospital as a trainee drug and substance abuse counsellor. The proximity of the Wandsworth base to the new apartment made it a really useful new home. Her experience with Eddie had forged a new ambition in her to prevent more lives from being ruined. Bronwen had finally left the Welsh hills and secured a job as a secondary teacher in a local school allowing commuting time to be kept to a minimum for both young women.

Today Georgina was carrying a large bag containing special offer champagne from the local Sainsbury's supermarket and a selection of ready made nibbles for a housewarming celebration. Her research grant had almost finished and her pocket money was supplemented by the occasional energy healing or psychic card reading amongst friends of friends. As she pushed the door open a large leg, seemingly attached to a parlour palm, pushed past her to hold the door wide open. Giles planted a big noisy kiss on top of her shiny blonde head as he leaned into the doorway to prop his size eleven Russell and Bromley shoe against the white double glazed door.

"Aha it is a jar, methinks," he said predictably. Georgina turned with surprise to give him a hello hug as she moved the large plant to one side.

"Wow, I thought you were a spy in the jungle, Giles. Nice to see you again. Have you moved South too?"

"Hello darling, no not yet but a whole lot of my body seems to have gone somewhat south recently!" Georgina chuckled as she led the way to the shiny new lift doors and pressed the button to wait.

"Is Ralph coming to help celebrate the new flat then ?" Giles grinned happily as he answered.

"Oh yes he will be along on his new Harley as soon as he finishes work, he is over this way today, selling houses to some wealthy Russians. They seem to be the only ones with any spare cash these days. When I said houses I meant that in the plural, he is getting amazing sales recently, hence the new bike."

"I love the smell of new buildings and fresh paint don't you?" Georgina moved into the spacious mirror lined lift as she spoke.

"I'm not so sure about new lifts though darling, I hope this has been well tested and that we are not going to spend a long night stuck half way between floors, still we could break open that bottle you have there, chilled or not I could lose my snobbery with some warm champers quite easily." Georgina laughed prettily.

"Honestly Giles you have some imagination, let's not even energise the thought. All will be perfect and just as it should be, I am sure."

"There you go already with that blessed positive motivational speak that you do so well." he chuckled as he added, "But I do have to thank you for all of the help that you gave to poor old Eddie in recent months. He really is a new man and he has willingly gone along to meetings with Ralph you know. In fact I believe he has been clean almost since your second session with him am I right?"

She coughed and looked away for a few seconds for Giles to realise that he may be invading some professional code or other. "Oh sorry, sweetie, I didn't mean to ask you to cross any ethical borders, I know he is doing well, because he is so proud of himself."

"No, no don't worry Giles of course he is doing well and responded immediately to my therapies so I am not speaking out of order. He loves everyone to know how he is doing and it actually seems to help him to be proud of his recovery by telling everyone he knows. I even heard him telling a teenager on the underground last week." She laughed at the memory of Eddie chatting to a tattooed youngster on the tube as she was strap hanging in the aisle a few steps away. She had been on her way to the printers with her newly completed thesis when she happened to board the same Northern Line train as Eddie. She had not made herself known to him because she was in her own little world as was often the case when she travelled in crowded trains. She knew that she needed to protect her energy field or she would see and hear what others were thinking. Not only that but other unwelcome energies could easily inveigle their way into her auric field. It was something she had needed to learn in her teens to protect herself because of her sensitive soul. She was happy to help others when it was needed but only when requested and properly organised. Without such protection she could end a day either physically and mentally drained or inundated with emotions that did not belong to her. She decided this was something she would not be sharing with the still skeptical Giles right now.

"He was giving this young guy a real lecture and sounded like a soldier again as he gave advice about not wasting your life no hard drugs or smoking weed. Life's too short to piss about don't ya know!" She grinned proudly as she skilfully imitated Eddie's words to a stranger. "This was all because he could smell pot smoke on the guy's clothes and as he had raised his tattooed arm to the strap he had exposed needle marks in his arm. Silly guy."

"I know I am a slightly different generation but I have never understood the need to trip out of your body, unless of course it's with a drop of the old falling down juice!" Giles smiled knowingly as he joked about his own love of strong martinis. "I have to say though I have honestly never lost control in that I couldn't remember when a good time was had by all. Wish I could say the same for dear Ralphie. He just didn't know when to stop and would have carried on drinking to oblivion until he saw the light, so to speak."

They had managed to wrestle themselves and the over sized plant out of the lift and onto the third floor corridor whilst they were chatting. The door to the new apartment was already open and music could be heard over chatter and giggles floating along the corridor towards them.

"Sounds like we are just in time to have a bit of "craic" as Kyrie would say." Giles mimicked Kyrie's Irish accent in a fond uncle kind of way. He really was a good friend to the Belfast woman who was at last finding her feet in mainland Britain after an uncertain start when she had landed, many years ago now, almost running, with her Welsh ex soldier lover beside her. It had not been easy for them. Giles was well aware that it had been Kyrie who had coped the best, finding herself a nannying job within weeks whist Eddie floundered in civilian life without the structure of military life to guide him. As if she had sensed his thoughts Kyrie bounced out of the door, her shiny dark hair flying behind her.

"At last! We thought you were lost so far south, gawd, is that a plant or a tree walking beside youse?"

The friends all chuckled together as Giles thrust the plant into her arms whilst kissing her through the fronds. Georgina waved the basket of food and drink at her as she too leaned into kiss Kyrie's already flushed cheek.

"Lead me to the bar darling." Giles commanded in his best thespian impersonation.

Bronwen came running across the light and airy living room that had been arranged to accommodate the eclectic collection of friends old and new for the house warming party. Kyrie's old neighbour, sixty year old Freda, was grinning flirtatiously whilst chatting to a tall younger man in jeans and white tee-shirt. He was one of the newly found neighbours who had also moved into the block recently.

"Whatever are you drinking Freda?" Georgina asked as she squeezed past her on the way to find a dish for the canapés in the kitchen. Freda waved the glass containing sticky brown liquid under her nose.

"Oh it's my favourite black Russian, brought the Tia Maria with me. Haven't had it in years, just thought I'd celebrate in style today Georgie. How are you doing these days?"

"I'm great thanks, back in a tick when I get these nibbles sorted. I see they've got loads out already but I'd better do my bit."

Freda turned to gaze once more at the guy next to her. She had just learned that his name was Guy and she was giggling at the chance to tell someone that she was talking to a guy called Guy. "So what do you do then gorgeous Guy?" she asked in what she hoped sounded her young and cool voice.

"I'm in radio, actually, sort of a boyhood ambition to combine war and acting." He was scanning the room above Freda's permed brassy blonde head as he spoke. He didn't mind passing time with the old dear but he really had come to check out the new hotties on the block. He dragged his smile back to Freda as she was asking a question again.

"War and acting what do you mean, are you a BBC war correspondent, funny I haven't seen or heard you I love all this Middle Eastern coverage?" Freda was screwing her face up trying to imagine his voice coming out of her radio. "Although I suppose it's not right to love war stuff!" she added just to cover up her gushing adulation that even she began to realise was not being received with any enthusiasm.

"No Freda, nothing as glamorous or as dangerous, I'm afraid. I work for BFBS, the Forces Broadcasting Service. It can be good occasionally if they send us off to do interviews. Budgets don't stretch to that much these days though. Pity, well, I'll just go and see can I help the new girl with the nibbles." He took his opportunity to escape to the small kitchen where Georgina was opening cupboards looking for serving dishes. Freda ambled over to the well worn settee that had made it from the old flat. It certainly could do with a good clean she thought as Georgina shot out of the kitchen at a rate of knots better suited to Fastnet yachts.

"What's up?" asked Kyrie as she went to her friend's side.

"Oh nothing." replied Georgina with pink cheeks and wide, slightly hazy eyes. "Just thought I would see if you want the champagne open now?"

"Yeah right," scoffed Bronwen as she joined her friends. "Nothing to do with Mr Cool in there then?" She tossed her head towards the kitchen door where Guy was just exiting by using his jean clad backside as he carried a dish of mini sausage rolls into the room.

"No, well not really, well a bit I suppose. I just saw someone with him that gave me a bit of a scare that's all. It's ok now really it is."

"Something I said ?" smiled Guy as he sauntered over to them, not believing his luck to have an audience of all the best looking young women at once. "Sausage roll anyone?"

Bronwen was searching for something sarcastic to say hoping to put this smoothie in his place, whilst Kyrie took the dish from him and patted his arm. "Thanks Guy you are well trained I can see." and she did her best eye lash flutter as she sashayed away towards another group of neighbours who were chatting to Eddie.

"I am so sorry Guy … I …" Georgina decided that some sort of explanation was needed as Bronwen interrupted.

"So you haven't heard about our Georgie then have you?" She was getting wide eyed head shaking from Georgina as she said this to Guy. But he turned towards her and asked:

"Now this sounds fascinating, tell me more, or wait, shall I get my tape recorder out and get a scoop or what?"

"No, it's just I wonder how you feel about the spirit world and outside energy fields Guy? It's not everyone that wants to talk about these things. Bronwen has known me a long time and she is used to me and the "other" things that I see sometimes."

"Sometimes!" scoffed Bronwen, "give me a break for Christ's sake!"

Guy had crossed his arms and was supporting his chin with one hand as he looked more carefully at the tiny blonde in front of him. She really did look as though she could be blown away like a feather. Her long hair was really shiny today as it settled on her shoulders before sliding gracefully down her back. He had the urge to stroke this delicate, gently inclined, head. She was looking at him with an expression of concern and the question remained in the air between them. Bronwen was trying not to think about his well worked biceps pushing out of the short white T shirt arms. She couldn't believe her luck that this Adonis was just down the hall from her new home. What a pity he only had eyes for Georgina right now. She was busily working out her next smart remark that either immediately hooked or repelled the previous men she had fancied.

"So what are you then, some kind of palm reader or psychic or what?" Guy was asking in a manner that suggested he was expecting it to be a joke of some kind.

"And some, you couldn't even start to imagine!" Bronwen took the liberty of nudging him in the ribs that were part of the six pack she had been admiring. She regretted it immediately as she often did with her over familiar style, kicking into play at all the wrong moments. His eyes never left Georgina.

"Palm reading is for fairgrounds, but yes I am psychic and have been all my life, for my sins. It is not always helpful in everyday life." She paused to see what effect this information was having on him. She had learned over the years that some could handle it with interest and others just wanted to run, laugh or be very rude to hide their fear. Guy was not sure how he felt about it but knew he didn't want this delicate young woman to go away just yet. He was also wondering how to lose the Welsh sidekick who was starting to get up his nose with her remarks and nudging.

Bronwen got the message and left them with a parting shot," You'd better believe boyo, it *is very helpful,* no matter what she says, I am a witness to the benefits." She managed to refrain from one last nudge on the delicious chest that she had been ogling and tried to copy Kyrie's sashaying hip movement. One day she would get it right, she hoped, as she swaggered away to join the others.

"So what just happened in the kitchen back there then, do I have B.O. or have I got a devil on my shoulder or what? I mean I know I can have an effect on girls but never quite like that before." He smiled what he hoped was his best intelligent but wistful look as he leaned his hip against the dining table where he had deposited the plate of sausage rolls.

"I'm not sure if you will want to hear this." She looked more closely into his eyes searching for a sign that he could handle what she was about to say. She carried on anyway with a deep breath as she felt that familiar tingle in her scalp that encouraged her to continue.

"I saw someone behind you."

"Go on" He interrupted, "Do I know this person or nonperson or spook or whatever you call them?"

"I'm not sure, he obviously wanted you to know he was there, but he came in so quickly I got a bit of a shock in a nice new apartment like this. In older buildings there are often trace energies from other times and spirits who have been hanging about, sort of, or angelic energy that has been helping someone before, no this was definitely for you. I am sorry I didn't stay focussed to get the message."

"So what did it, sorry, he, look like?"

"That's the problem, I didn't get a real facial energy, but he was hanging by what looked like a school tie from the ceiling and I just saw and felt his pain."

Guy slumped down onto the dining chair that was luckily just behind him, "Oh God!"

Georgina put her hand on his shoulder as she squatted down in front of him. "Does that mean you know who it was?"

"It must be my old mate from the sixth form, he hanged himself in the locker room before rugby practise, he couldn't take the ribbing anymore. They always annoyed him when he took his kit off to play a match." He was rubbing his hand over his brow to try to cover his eyes and stem the tears that were welling up behind his lids. "You see he was gay, but had never officially come out and the other lads knew, but just wanted to goad him into saying something. He had been my best mate since primary school, I should've been able to stand up for him, but you know that machismo teenage crap that lads force at school?"

She was nodding sympathetically, "Not only in the teenage years, unfortunately."

He started to look furtively around the room to check who was listening to his words, satisfied that everyone else was having fun and fully occupied in other conversations with full glasses and nibbles in hands, he continued to share his story with Georgina.

"I always felt guilty that I didn't help him more, but to be honest I didn't know what else I could do. I was often accused of being gay too. Funnily enough that never annoyed me, I guess I was centred in my own sexuality by then ." He paused to give this full effect on the cute girl who was looking at him with such concern and empathy. He certainly didn't want her to think he batted for the other side. "We hung out together when we didn't have partners, actually I don't think he had ever really had sex, just some fumbling outside the flicks and things like that, so sad really he was a great bloke. He deserved a helluva lot more from life."

"Well, listening to this I think he just came along today to say thanks and let you know that it was nothing to do with you. That is mostly why such spirits come back when I am around, they either want to say they love you or they are sorry or both, of course. I wouldn't dwell on it any more he will know we have had this chat and we can just send your love to him so that he can get on and do whatever he has to do now on the other side." Georgina stood up to ease her aching thighs that had become numb in the squatting position resting uncomfortably as she was on her high heeled boots.

"But it was a long time ago now, I'm 28 so it must be 10 years at least since he went. Does that mean he has been waiting all these years to communicate with me, just hanging around." He chuckled at this pun as he realised what he had said. Georgina too was giggling as she replied,

"No you have to know that time has no meaning once we are out of the earth's physical field so it will have been only like moments for him as he will have been fully occupied doing whatever it is they do when they pass over. Suicide, I am told, is always a little different for the soul when it passes and there may be all kinds of other life reviews they have to go through to make sure they learn the lessons that they were sent to that particular body to learn. I find it all fascinating, but we have to remember we are here on earth to live, love and enjoy alongside the learning so lets not get too preoccupied with death and disaster, you know?" She leaned over to fill his glass from the wine bottle on the table beside them. He stood up to chink his glass to hers and at the same time he shook his shoulders as though to remove some tingling energy that had collected around them.

"I'm all for that loving and enjoying bit, noo doubt about it." She too shrugged her shoulders as she chinked her glass to his and turned to smile at Eddie who was walking towards them. He waved his orange juice glass at them, to show how abstemious he was being.

"Hi Doc what are you two up to? With all that shoulder shaking you look like a couple of wet dogs. Must be something weird and wonderful going on in this corner?" He winked at Guy and extended his hand "Eddie Gethin, how're ye doing?"

Guy shook the Welsh man's hand with more gusto than normal, trying to shake off the remnants of the surreal interactions he had just had with Georgina. A bit of male bonding could be what he needed right then. "Doc! Are you a Medic then ?" He turned to Georgina with raised eyebrows. "I thought you were a palm reader and spooky girl not a professional person?"

She sighed with resignation as she realised that yet again someone had not really listened to anything she had said once the psychic phenomena had been discussed. He had taken what he needed from the discussion, offloaded his guilt and reverted immediately to denigrating what had just been explained to him. "Yeah right, I suppose that is just what I am. Science plays a big part in what I do and 10 years of worldwide research came into play somewhere along the line but for most people it's a game or mumbo jumbo no matter how I explain, never mind. Enjoy your evening Guy, nice meeting you. Catch you later Eddie." She moved swiftly off to chat with her friends, leaving a bemused Guy to look at Eddie with raised shoulders and arms out to mime a what did I do ? expression.

"Fucked that up eh boyo?"

"I don't understand, she never said she was a doctor, tell me what I did wrong. Oh I know, she may have told me something about a school friend that died but anyone could've done that who knew me, perhaps she heard from one of the neighbours, 'cos I always talk about my old school mate who killed himself you know?"

Eddie slipped his arm around Guy's shoulders.

"Don't feel too bad. She is well used to it but she really is a very special young woman and deserves more respect. Her PhD was in Cosmic energy and Angels or something like that, can't remember, but I do know she knows her stuff and has looked at "spooky stuff" as you call it from all over the world. Seems there is a lot more proof out there than any of us were allowed to believe for centuries. I haven't actually read her thesis but all I know is she sorted me out big time when I was in my last chance saloon." He waved the orange juice under Guy's nose as he said this.

"Drink problems?"

"No, much more than that mate, p'raps I could've dealt with the booze. No, I was into the class A gear and, well you don't want to know really, 'cause I didn't even admit to myself what I was up to."

"Ex squaddie right?" Guy's professional instincts came into play almost immediately.

"How did you know? It has been a long time now since I took the Queen's silver."

Guy smiled and tapped the side of his nose with one finger. "Just an instinct from a few years of doing interviews for BFBS radio programmes. Something in the way you carry yourselves and the odd turn of *matey* phrase, you know what I mean?"

"Yes I know, it seems to get ingrained and I reckon it's what causes problems for us in civvy street. A whole way of life and a comradeship that we never seem to find again, or at least don't allow ourselves to find again. Georgina allowed me chance to have a real look at who I was inside, if that doesn't sound too daft?"

He turned to scan the room checking for eavesdroppers. He found himself warming to this guy called Guy who was obviously a trained listener and nodded in all the right places to encourage him to continue. "I had tried conventional detox programmes a few years ago and I always drifted back to scoring, starting with the odd spliff with the booze and then the rest followed naturally each time. It was seeing Kyrie (my ex) getting on with her life over here, she came from Northern Ireland with me when I left the forces, that really made me feel a bit useless, I guess. Anyway it was Georgie who helped me look deeper into why I did it and I got a few shocks when I started to delve deeper."

"What kind of shocks?" Guy patted Eddie's arm to show his interest and sympathy. "I mean, I'm sorry I don't mean to pry if you would rather not give me any details, my reporter's nose always gets the better of me."

"No mate, it's fine, I tell everyone 'cos it was such a relief and it all happened so quickly once I trusted myself to get on with it. I had done all that conventional shit with twelve step programmes and the rest, it did help some of my mates but I just went off the rails too easily as soon as I got excited by something, like a job interview, new girl or whatever. Georgie helped me into my own energy field so that I could really see why I kept repeating the same old life patterns. She should be a shrink, she is so good at it."

Guy was looking very interested now but asked in a tetchy voice showing his frustration. "Yes but what did she *do* ?"

"I think you could say a bit of everything, she calls it energy medicine with deep meditation and spiritual input. I really went into a floaty state where her questions then guided me into my childhood and then away back into other past lives, weird or what?"

"So she made suggestions to you that helped?" Guy was trying to understand but starting to feel a bit scornful of what sounded crackers to him.

"No she never made any *suggestions* at all she just listened to me as I talked about what I saw, how I felt, where I was. Honestly, I couldn't have made it up if you'd asked me to tell a story, I went to places you just couldn't imagine from this life right now. She recorded it all so when we listened back together I could analyse it myself and we discussed some things that didn't seem to be from past lives at all but just from *ME*. It sounds odd when I retell it but I was walking on water at one stage in this meditation and I thought if she tries to tell me I was bloody Jesus then I will crack up!"

"And?" Guy really wanted to know more, amused by Eddie's down to earth story telling of what sounded incredible.

"We decided it was a sign to show me that I can do whatever I want in this life if I have faith in myself." He was laughing now as he got into the incredulity of it all. "I mean, how simple is that? She called it a conceptualisation, seems she gets the same kind of pictures from spirits, the dead guys, you know that come to help her give messages to us lot down here. A bit like her seeing your dead mate, tonight, I suppose. Anyway, whatever, it works for me and I don't give a shit what people think, 'cause as far as I'm concerned I feel the strongest and happiest I have been for many years. I could bore the boxers off you if I went into all the lives I saw that showed me how I had learned to become dependent on outside stimulation of one kind or another over many lifetimes. Just believe me it worked and very quickly too, once I got the message. Cheers mate!" He raised his glass and chinked the empty wine glass being held up by a bemused looking Guy.

"I think I owe that girl an apology and what can I say to you? Just damn good job, well done, err ..., fuck me, I feel a bit dazed by it all.

Guy sank down once more onto the dining chair beside him as he tried to process his thoughts after all that Eddie had recounted. Was there anyone normal in the room right now he wondered. His eyes lit on the bright and brassy Freda as she threw her head back to laugh loudly at something being said by Giles. *Thank Christ normality*, he hoped. Giles wandered away from Freda to the door as another good looking, well dressed man walked in carrying a bike helmet and a soft leather jacket. Guy watched as the two men embraced and Ralph handed over his biker kit to his partner. Eddie was already carrying another glass of orange juice towards Ralph.

"Here we go matey, I've been saving the good stuff for us two, we seem to be the only tee totallers here tonight. How's business?"

Ralph clapped his arm around Eddie's shoulders. It was an interesting interaction between the two men looking so different with the rough, tough ex soldier and the sophisticated, genteel estate agent obviously pleased to see each other in a natural man hug.

Ralph looked every bit the biker when on his Harley scooting through the streets of London and the home counties, but the minute he climbed off the bike his gait and soft facial features proudly showed the world that he was in touch with his feminine side. He had a tiny goatee beard that Giles kept neatly trimmed for him and his sandy coloured hair was still full and tended to curl at the bottom if it was not kept short. He liked the slight quiff that fell over his forehead to allow him to flick it at appropriate times when he wished to make a point in conversation. Giles, always ready to fix life for them both had a tendency to say "Don't do that dear it is soo gay!" For now Guy was lost in a between worlds area of thought and everything appeared in slow motion and slightly surreal to someone who was more used to chatting down the line to military types in the world's trouble spots and their families who fretted about their safety from home.

Bronwen bounced into his vision as she helped herself to wine from the bottle on the table beside him. "Can I pour you another one handsome?"

"Oh sure, yes please, I need one, I feel a bit overwhelmed with the chat I've had so far tonight!" He was actually pleased to see her again and hoped she had no more spooky tales or energy phenomena to share with him right now.

"Yep, my pals are a weird and wonderful bunch, well that's just Georgina actually. In fact she is the only one, but she does seem to be having an effect on many different people recently. Sort of coming into her own, so to speak."

He grinned at her boyishly. "You can say that again, I am having real trouble getting to grips with reality right now. Who would've thought that cute little blond could have so much inside her or around her or wherever it all comes from. At the moment I can't quite handle it all. My morning show will bring me down to earth though with any luck."

Bronwen was perching on the table looking down at him slumped in his chair and thought that he didn't look down to earth at all, more like some kind of Greek God in jeans. "So tell me about your show, does everyone who rings in have to be a military type then?" She didn't really care but just wanted to engage him in any conversation that kept his mind off Georgina, much as she loved her, she didn't think she deserved all the good looking men.

Kyrie and Georgina were in the kitchen discussing the finished dissertation that Georgina needed to get published as soon as she could. "I know it needs published for a bigger audience so I have an appointment with the publishers next week, it all takes so much time and I need to get on and earn some money to make up for all the research travel money I spent. Mam and dad were great but really at my age I should be contributing a bit more to society and making some money."

"No time to worry about that now Georgie, you have a life mission that's one thing I know and it will all fit into place for you. Gawd, look what you have done to help people already, you should've been charging for all the fixing you have done with our friends and acquaintances. Listen to me I'm starting to sound like you, you will never know how much you have helped me get onto a new life path. This new job, the new flatmate, thanks to you and a whole new way of being, Yep it really is getting to be an interesting life alright."

"Yeah I am just happy you two hit it off so well. Moving down here was a really good move. You may find me on your settee the odd night until I see what I am doing and where I am doing it." Kyrie was nodding happily at this, thinking of the fun the three girls could have together with wine bars and cinemas all within walking distance of their new nest. Georgina was continuing,

"I just wish you had time to come to the Mind Body Spirit exhibition with me next week, I have a good feeling about it for some reason. I'm also wondering if I can get along to the Hay House "You Can Do It" conference it sounds so interesting. The speakers are all inspirational and they quote a lot of the scientific evidence that I have used in my thesis, it's always good to have it corroborated in a public presentation."

Kyrie, anxious to get back to earth, put her arm round her friend's shoulders, "Georgie the whole of our life feels interesting right now, I mean have you seen the hunks who live round here?" They walked back to join the party giggling and still discussing what could be interesting in the weeks ahead.

They were to see just how interesting in a very short time. The escalator was starting off slowly but there would be more than them on it as life worked it's magic in more ways than one.

Chapter 10

Aramantha and the Psychiatrist

Az found herself being peered at through castled fingers with the navy blue linen clad elbows of the psychiatrist resting firmly on an expensive desk. She found herself wondering about the best line of response to take with this young man who was reputed to be the newest whizz kid taking London by storm with his miraculous treatment for all kinds of phobias and neurotic behaviour.

The designer stubble that was now resting on the castled finger tips really made her want to offer some new razor blades to Doctor Jordan. He could be my son, she thought with horror. He was doing that quiet, kindly stare practised by some therapists hoping that it will encourage the client to talk. As she returned his smile she realised that he had been asking a question.

"I'm sorry?"

"I was asking how long you have been hearing voices?"

"Well, I was wondering how long you have been practising as a psychiatrist But I think it must be eight years since you started to specialise in London, after your medical degree from Newcastle - am I right?"

"Yes you are exactly right! How did you know?"

"Oh just a wee voice in my head."

Now came that benign smile and slight shake of the head as Dr Jordan tried not to laugh out loud.

"Yes well, Aramantha, I understand that the voice seems real to you and of course you will have looked up my credentials before booking the appointment I am sure."

"Are you?"

"What?"

"Sure." The young man stroked his carefully coiffed chin before replying in what he hoped was a professional manner, "well that's what most of my new clients seem to do."

"Ah yes but you see I am not normal as in the term "most new clients" would suggest, I have always had a problem with conforming to social norms- Didn't my husband tell you?"

"Well he ..."

"I rarely use a computer, they tend to blow up around me you see, and if I did I am sure there are far more interesting facts that I could research."

"Now Mrs Raven I never discuss my patients with anyone else outside of this room, I .."

Az continued as if he had not spoken, feeling suddenly empowered.

"For instance if you just looked at a few research papers in the area of quantum physics or quantum mechanics you will see that many findings are being reported as completely counter intuitive, outside of the everyday experiential norm but they cannot be denied. For example research with light particles are being pushed to the limits and the results are quite astounding to the uninitiated. Social psychologists are taking on board psychic phenomena, some medics are even using energy healing, psychic healing and most neurologists are now very willing to state that they do not know what consciousness is, or even how it is generated but psychic research is starting to show that we can measure thought patterns and even perhaps the soul energy or electromagnetic field of the living organism so that is the kind of thing I would like to study more should I have time to spend on a computer. Which I don't!"

As she paused for breath, she suddenly realised that she felt quite light headed at this outburst. On further reflection she decided that she was more euphoric than faint and would like to go on. The time spent planning her strategy with Lyre had been invaluable. She did wonder though had she over stepped the mark with this relatively young professional.

Dr. Jordan was trying hard to maintain his professional calm as his middle aged patient suddenly seemed to be glowing before him. "You know Aramantha, it is easy to read a few New Age ideas and be influenced by them, especially if one is feeling a little vulnerable, shall we say? When we hear voices it can be caused by a number of different factors, not meaning that you are insane or mad in common parlance."

"Firstly doctor, I am not in the least concerned that I may be considered "mad," as you say and I do not believe "we" *are* hearing voices at all as you obviously are not really listening to what I am trying to explain to you so that makes one of us who is not hearing any voices at all really, doesn't it?"

"I can understand your reluctance to address these problems Aramantha, I am well aware that our mind can play tricks on us and that everything is possible with brain activity registering fantasising as a real phenomenon. Especially, may I add, if you are feeling a bit down or depressed, perhaps preparing for that empty nest syndrome when your daughter graduates?"

Az decided not to respond to what she felt to be patronising provocation when fantasising was mentioned. She decided instead to re shape her information for Dr. Jordan's benefit.

"You know that all truths that are initially hard to deal with, inevitably go through three distinct stages in cognition and public discussion? First it is ridiculed (as in those who first said that the world was round). Then it is vehemently opposed (as in the medieval authorities who imprisoned Galileo for making public his new astronomy work). Then it is accepted as really true because of the evidence and suddenly the disclaimers melt into the background as though they had known something was true all along. In fact I can refer you to a well known psychotherapist who I met years ago at a London presentation by a good friend of mine and he assured me that he didn't believe in any of this energy mumbo jumbo as his clients 'expected more of him'. Hah!

Actually I now see that he has recognised the growing trends and calls himself a 'holistic practitioner' nowadays, holistically swelling his bank balance I presume."

She suddenly decided that she could not let the fantasy taunt go without adding,

"Further more, I know that work done with electro encephalograms shows that fantasising does not have the same cortical-to-subcortical shift in brain activity as does an altered state of consciousness that allows access to psychic activity in the human mind. Incidentally if we start to play with the semantics of what a mind actually is we could have many expensive discussion sessions in this office couldn't we?"

At this point the handsome young shrink decided he may have bitten off a bit more than he could chew with this client and he coughed to give himself thinking time. Another idea suddenly came to him that could get the control back into his therapeutic remit.

"I don't want you to think I have a closed mind to all that you are saying, but I do know that schizophrenia has a genetic link, and your husband tells me that your mother also had some delusional tendencies because..."

"Ok, that's it, I am sorry but I cannot sit here and listen to this piffle, first you tell me that you don't discuss clients outside and then you tell me you listen to uninformed, misguided information from my husband who loved my mother, or so he said, in the early years of our relationship because she was seen as eccentric, outspoken and fun. Now you are quite unprofessionally making a gross assumption that someone who you never met was in some way schizophrenic- in the parlance of my daughter – Give me a break Doctor Jordan." Victor Jordan was decidedly uncomfortable at this response.

He retorted, "It's just that it is probable, psychologically speaking, for people with some kind of mental disturbance to express repressed emotions of one kind another by imagining spiritual input from no valid input."

"My goodness you must have read the old committee report from those crusty Archbishops commissioned to look at spiritualism, I seem to think that they said something similar away back in 1937. They did eventually agree that psychic phenomena could be real, but went into such detail that the report was banned for over nine years. Can you imagine that? There is so much that we could agree upon if the inherent fear that is oddly similar in scientific and church groups were to be disected. Pity!"

Az was gathering her Chanel bag and Sarah Moon raw silk jacket from the chair as she headed towards the door. The Young psychiatrist started to follow her across the room when she abruptly turned and put her hand up towards him. He stopped as if struck by the force of energy that came between them. If he had not known better he would have thought that she had sent an electrical stun ray towards him, as seen on those American police documentary programmes. She saw his bewilderment and suddenly she remembered Lyre's advice and decided to take pity on his lack of understanding. After all he was very young and relatively inexperienced. He was certainly very good looking, her daughter would have described him as "well fit"! Perhaps she had a job to do after all.

"Look, I know we have not got off to a very good start, but I really think we have things to learn from each other, even help each other as best we can. Plus, I know that my husband is willing to pay as much as it takes to make me more, shall we say, socially acceptable? You may as well benefit financially as well as giving me a regular self indulgent opportunity to talk about myself for a refreshing change. What do you say that we book another session and start over?"

Victor Jordan, looked at this still attractive middle aged woman who had so intrigued his professional mind with the very different energy that she had brought to his consulting room. First the "glow" that had seemed to cover her whole body and yet he was no longer certain that he had seen it, and now the bolt of energy that had so recently met him across the room, as he walked towards her at the doorway. The idea of a regular income from a well healed client never went amiss either.

"You have a deal Aramantha, please make an appointment with my secretary as you leave and I look forward to our next meeting." He extended his hand as she took a step back towards him and smiled her agreement.

He was still smiling somewhat bemusedly as he held his own hand and tried to assess why the warmth from her handshake had lasted until long after Az had descended in the glass lift from his expensive office foyer. He acknowledged that as intensive as his studies had been, his thirst for new horizons allowed him to know he had a lot to learn in many aspects of his life, both professionally and personally. Maybe she was right maybe there was some reciprocal learning in this new client- doctor relationship. Whatever it was that had caused the energy in his office to vibrate in a very different way he wanted to know more, and if he could help this intriguing woman whilst he himself did some research then it would be a bonus. He was already googling 1937 reports about The Church of England and Spiritualism.

Chapter 11

Georgina and Lyre

Looking at the façade of the old mansion with its mixture of baroque architecture and Georgian features Georgina became excited by the real sense of history in this rural idyll. Her invitation to attend this interesting little soiree came from Lyre an older woman she had recently met. At least she thinks that she is older because her energy feels younger than she looks. As Lyre parked her beaten up Volkswagen Beetle in the field designated as a car park for the evening Georgina had time to wonder what she was doing there with a relatively new acquaintance in a quite isolated place and about to meet a group about whom she knew absolutely nothing.

As the stately, elegant, Lyre floated towards her on a perfumed cloud of frankincense and lavender she felt safe and protected for reasons she was beginning to understand deep in her soul. Why had she just walked up to Lyre in the Mind Body Spirit festival in London only a month ago? Something had attracted her to the aura around this tall slim woman of uncertain age. To say she glowed would be an exaggeration but she certainly gave out a warm light of what could only be called loving energy. In fact she wasn't even certain if she had walked up to her or if she had been summoned in an esoteric cloud of energy. Lyre was doing angel and intuitive card readings in a small booth that had a queue of hopefuls waiting patiently along the perimeter. She was not dressed like so many of the stereotypical card readers in purple velvet and headbands and dangling earrings. She looked just like a sophisticated professor having dinner with friends. Her simple black dress was from Armani and her jewellery was handmade from real crystals of rose quartz, amethyst and labradorite. The simple diamond pins in her ears twinkled in the lights of the room. The hair do was somewhat different with the Cruella DeVille twist and the neatly trimmed back swept smoothly up to a distinctly coloured black and white up swept fringe.

When Georgina wandered past the stall Lyre called out to her, "Do you know that even Aristotle taught that the seat of human consciousness lies not in the brain but in the heart?"

"I'm sorry?" replied Georgina, somewhat stunned by this call. "Is it me you're speaking to?

"Well if it's not you then I have just seen the wrong energy field rippling past me, are you called Georgie or George or something like that?"

"Yes almost, Georgina, that's who I am, Georgina!"

"Of course you are. Please, do come and sit down dear girl, that's if you have time?

"I thought that Aristotle would reach you – he always does. You see I'm sure you know that the magnetic field produced by the heart is more than five thousand times greater in strength than the field generated by the brain, *and* it can be detected at least five feet from the body in all directions. I actually disagree with the scientists on this point and think it goes on out into the Universe for millenniums in light years. That's why I could feel your energy as you were walking past over there. You have wonderful heart energy. You must have been told that before? It made me look up, but I was already being prompted, from another dimension, to speak to you."

Georgina was looking both amazed and excited by now, "But what do they want from me?" The waiting queue of on lookers were now riveted to the interaction that was taking place between the two women. Nudges and whispers rippled through the group of men and women who no longer seemed to be annoyed by what appeared to be a queue jumper. What did *who* want from her and who were "they"?

"Do you feel that you are working at your full potential right now?"

"I suppose that's why I came along today, just because I feel myself drifting again. This often happens to me when I am waiting for a new door to open. I thought that once I had finished the thesis for my PhD all would fit into place but it doesn't seem to be the case."

"You have to know that full potential is *not* reached by not working with our emotions properly. If we are not in tune with our emotional body and not sharing our emotions coherently with self and others then we are out of balance. Your light body is essential to reaching your full potential, understanding our electromagnetic nature is a key area for your work, *and* I do believe that you haven't published your final thesis have you?"

"How did you know? But you are right, I suppose I *am* quite a private person. I don't know whether I am ready for all of that publicity that may happen when I publish."

"I personally think that private is not a word that we can use as light workers, nor as anyone who wants to participate in the real society of earth people. Emotions generate frequencies that the heart field can transmit as information to be received by others."

"I understand that, but I don't think my personal feelings are important to anyone else."

Georgina shifted in the exquisite cherry wood side chair that was facing Lyre across a beautifully carved cherry wood pedestal table. The furniture used by Lyre in her booth was always delivered from her home for these exhibitions. Today she had chosen a 1715 Queen Anne pedestal table with a top burnished and polished to perfection. The cards were able to slide across the shiny top to her side as they were chosen by each client. Lyre was sitting in the matching carved wooden framed chair to Georgina's with the added comfort of wooden arms. Her concession to the esoteric ambience was that they were both covered in a deep pile purple velvet. The addition of an enormous clear quartz crystal forming a centre piece completed the elegant difference of this booth.

Lyre continued to speak soothingly to her new friend as though quietening a skittish colt.

"That is where you are so very misguided, about your personal emotions. The electromagnetic field generated by the heart is modulated by different emotional states. We are receiving each others energy whether we realise or not and that is where we have a responsibility to our self and other people and even to the greater group consciousness. You must have learned that during your research surely?"

"Wow, and I thought I was just dropping in here to have a look around and now look what I'm getting, I just love this!" As she said it Georgina was not so sure that she did love it.

"Balance is achieved electromagnetically between mind, body and soul. Human potential is a combination of physical health, psychic abilities, creativity, mental and physical prowess all wrapped up in a package of energy. But you know all this." Lyre leaned back in her seat as if she felt that she was getting too intense and needed to take the pressure off this pretty young woman.

"This is so funny because I read that Aldous Huxley stated that facts do not cease to exist because they are ignored and I have been ignoring quite a lot of things of late, not least my own emotions. I can feel – or at least have long been aware of electrical charges around me that I cannot always explain." Georgina looked around her rather furtively as if checking out who was listening.

"Do you know that I had a visit from a wonderful loving energy field dressed in really cool modern clothes, just when I needed him during my final thesis write up?"

"So etheric Eoin has already paid his visit. I am sure he was really helpful to you? He and I have had many previous lives together, not all of them as celibate as this one Mmm! In fact you were also with us in at least two of those old lives."

The cool Lyre looked almost girly and cute as her eyes went into her thoughts high in the ceiling chandeliers. The crowd that had now gathered were becoming entranced by the whole conversation and chatting amongst themselves in agreement or dissension as the mood took them.

Lyre decided that she had better get on with the day job and read some cards for fee paying clients, many of whom returned to this exhibition each year just to hear her words of wisdom.

"Look Georgina, I think we have lots to discuss, you and I, so why don't you take my card and give me a ring when you get chance. You may even like to come with me to a big circle that is happening in a couple of weeks time."

It was difficult for the now enthralled Georgina to rise from the chair, to leave the very stylishly decorated stand in central London's biggest MBS show with this interesting woman. She had a feeling of being at home with Lyre although they had never met before, at least not in this life, she was now starting to realise.

"Oh, OK, yes I will. It has been a real pleasure to meet you Miss er …?"

"My name is Lyre, everyone calls me just that. I am named after a medieval musical instrument, sad really because I can't reproduce a note with my own voice, in fact I clear a room when I try. I look forward to your call. You can ring any evening this week as I am in town for the show and try to keep the evenings free. As you can imagine, it is quite exhausting channelling messages and advising all day here. One of my lessons this time around is to learn to put in the boundaries. I don't always get it right."

The crowd parted and watched as Georgina floated away deep in her own thoughts, still not quite sure what had just happened.

"Ring me- don't forget, ring me. Oh and get that thesis published!" Lyre's voice cut through her mystic bubble across the crowd as the younger woman nodded absently mindedly to herself.

Georgina wandered off to see what other mysteries may be unveiled in this large exhibition centre that brought together so many different professional and pseudo professional therapists under one roof annually. She clutched the embossed business card in her hand and was not surprised to see and feel a tiny amethyst crystal embedded into one corner.

A few weeks later found Georgina walking, with Lyre, up to a rather grand Palladian oak door that could tell a few stories if only they had time to listen or rather feel who had touched it's mottled surface over the decades. The door was opened in the way of the best horror movies with un oiled bolts and hinges squealing as the interior came into view. The face that smiled out at them was beautiful and full of welcoming smiles. It topped a small cuddly woman's body in a bright green silk shift dress. The silk skimmed over ample curves and appeared to get hitched up in awkward ridges where it couldn't skim any more.

"Az!"

"Hello Lyre, I'm so pleased you could come. I can tell you there are some right weirdoes here tonight. I need your down to earth support so much right now." Tall and stately Lyre bent down happily to scoop the shorter woman into her arms. The colours of their two silk dresses blended beautifully like a Gauguin painting. They parted to allow Lyre to introduce Georgina to Aramantha. "Ah, so this is the lovely Georgina! It is a pleasure to meet you at last." beamed Az.

"Thank you, I hope Lyre hasn't said too many bad things about me or something that I can't live up to."

"Oh no, Lyre has said nothing. In fact I was not even sure that she would be here until I heard that beetle engine chugging up the drive. I was so excited that's why I ran to let you in. It was just as I was reaching for the door handle that I heard them tell me that you were with her."

"Now Az, don't terrify the girl before she gets settled down." But Georgina was far from terrified as she looked at this beautiful woman who was snuggling into her side as she clutched her arm by the elbow. Everything felt just as it should be and she knew that there were interesting times ahead for her between these two friends. She was also beginning to realise that she had known them both before. All was about to become clear, as they say.

Lyre was explaining how she had managed to make contact with Georgina at the Mind Body Spirit exhibition in London and that they had met for coffee and in depth discussion on several occasions since that time. They had covered a lot of ground (or ether as the case may be) in a short time. They had explored their past lives and their connection to Eoin and Aramantha too. Whole books and presentations would be based on their previous connections in the years to come.

"Have you heard from Eoin recently Lyre?" Az asked from over her shoulder as she guided Georgina along a corridor decorated with guilt framed oil paintings, portraits of ancestors from different centuries. Lyre was pausing to investigate an artist's signature but turned to join them with two easy strides, her long legs making short work of the corridor. Az was already puffing slightly with excitement and effort, her chubby girth always causing her heart to work over time to get the oxygen into her lungs. Although she appeared to be propelling Georgina along, Georgina herself suspected that she was actually using her to keep upright as she felt her weight leaning on her elbow.

"Yes we spoke just yesterday and he, too, is very interested by Georgina's presence in our lives now. It is quite sad that it often takes so many years before we can rediscover our ancient connections in each new lifetime. I know that Eoin has a bit of a "thing" about this topic right now. He is muttering about the need to discuss with higher energies why we continually deprive our new borns of their hard earned inner wisdom from past lives. Always the campaigner that's our Eoin. He is also somewhat concerned about what may or may not be here tonight."

"What or who?" Az said mysteriously with a wicked glint in her eyes.

"Good point! Let's go see who we know."

Chapter 12

James

This guy really thinks that staying on top of his game has been mostly due to his personal charm. Self help books could have been written about his life. He is the young man who just got up one day and said "I want to work in the media." Although at that time he was already in a sort of media, a local newspaper in small town Wales, but that was not where he intended to stay till the grey and curlies were all over him. Although, he had never said no to grey haired ladies in positions of power, if they could help him along his path. He knew what he wanted and that was to be in London, in Television and preferably very well known. He had decided many years ago that he just did not do mediocre any more.

That first step had been to send off his C.V. to anywhere he could think of in the television field. He reluctantly acknowledged that he was no oil painting but he had a quirky kind of appeal that women seemed to respond to and men don't want to punch too much. He was non threatening in a sexy kind of way. At least that's what he thought when he looked in his circular, fully lit shaving mirror. He was slightly above average height. Tall enough to look superior when he chose. His thick springy hair was prematurely grizzled with a distinguished grey that he told himself added an air of intelligence. When he smiled, which wasn't often, the world shone for whoever was the recipient. Several young women had worked hard to secure just one smile from his thin lips.

There had been a fair share of love affairs but nothing or no one had ever sufficiently excited him more than his career. In fact "love affairs" should be translated as "shag pals." He had even admitted to his therapist that he had never loved anyone more than himself. The therapist was hired as a necessary peripheral to what he considered a famous media celeb would need in the years to come.

There was no rapport between them, professional or otherwise, but it was his insurance policy against failure. He was always wary of the old social norms from his Welsh mining genes, deep within his soul, in the form of his mother's voice ; "You can stop those airs and graces now bach"! The one he did consider more than most was "Be careful who you step on when going up the ladder, because you may need them on the way down."

Not that James had any intention of going down in his career he was committed to climbing quickly and as painlessly as possible. He knew that he was good at what he did and had the ability to make the right connection to the people that he interviewed. His first real break came when he was offered an anchor job in a serious news department. They liked the fact that he could look sincere even when all he really wanted to do was get out for the first pint of the night. His colleagues were admittedly mostly the wine bar or G & T types but they tolerated his working class drinking habits. What really bugged him was that he was supposed to do serious interviews with the political leaders and make like he didn't know that they were only as good as the civil servants who guide them, no matter which party was in power. The fact that several of these "guides" drink the same brand of beer as James was a big help in finding out more behind the scenes information to get the advance preparation the way that suited him. His cut throat style of interview became both feared and revered, depending upon who was on the receiving end. There was no doubt that James was both bright and dedicated to the job.

There was also a slightly caring side to his interviewing technique when a real human interest story came up. He particularly liked those "rags to riches" or "local boy rescues granny" kind of themes where he could look empathetically into the camera at strategic times.

The non political lead that was bugging him right now was what he termed "this new age stuff" about 2012 and the world ending because we're all sinners or whatever other bunkum he thought that the happy clappy, tree huggers were putting about. His sources were telling him that there was a group of psychics, spooky healers or fortune tellers holding some kind of séance in a rather grand country house in Wiltshire. He had heard that those who attended were offering god knows what to the devil take 'em philosophers in the London overspill areas. His producer was suggesting that he should get himself invited to see what was happening down there in rural anonymity. He was concerned that Jack, the producer, didn't seem to realise that he had a professional reputation to think about as a serious journalist.

He started to imagine the weirdoes that he was going to meet when he arrived and he was not sure if he could keep a straight face when they started all that daft, claptrap with crystal balls or whatever. There was, though, the remnants of the Welsh miner's boy telling him that odd things happened to people who dabbled in the occult! He well remembered being told not to go into the garish tent at the local fair where Gypsy Rose Marwhyn was offering her services for a palm full of silver. His teenage peers used to bet each other to see who dare go into her tent. They were never able to agree on whether young Dai Jones really did get more than his palm read. His broad smile and red face, topping his pulled back shoulders as he swaggered out of the tent suggested that perhaps she was more than useful to 14 year old virgin boys, but no one else dare to see for themselves. Oh yes, he knew about this stuff of old. He had already made contact with the guy who seemed to be organising it and cleared his attendance as an observer. He seemed a sane enough person who worked in a bank in Swindon, how unorthodox could he be?

It was being held on a cool summer evening and when he looked out of the office window he saw the storm clouds already gathering. He felt the same grey clouds in his head as he considered all of the other things he could be doing with his evening. There was the cute new researcher in the newsroom who gave him those sultry looks from under lashes that reminded him of the calf in the field next to his old family home. He used to to stroke the wet slippery nose as the calf licked his boyish hand. His adult hand could think of many better things to do when these sexy young lashes fluttered in his direction. Or there was the new play on at the Haymarket, his mates had tickets and a champagne reception on offer. The boy from the valleys had certainly expanded his social scene in recent years. Although he still knew that something was missing when he came down from the beer and champagne highs, no matter who he woke up next to.

Jack was still talking when he refocussed on the dusk filled office that was starting to get dark as the London sky continued to blacken over shepherds bush.

"I just know that we have the makings of a really good debate programme here. It seems to be in vogue, well zombies and vampires are. If you could find any of them it would be a bonus." He sniggered in a knowing way as his thoughts expanded the idea into his words. "Anyway, I can wheel out all the old cynics and loonies that we have spoken to over the years and then if you can find a few more weirdoes in Wiltshire we'll get ourselves a controversial rating that will set the switch boards alight. Love it - just up our street."

James suggested that a great example of all this esoterism that goes with spooks, the after life and reincarnation was the recent announcement that perhaps the Dalai Lama shouldn't be allowed to reincarnate and must chose a successor himself before he pops his clogs. "So where does that leave us?" Jack was shaking his head. "Hello your Holiness are you the reincarnation of yourself or are you the one chosen by your dead self, before you actually died or some other dead deity? Then these spiritual types wonder why we don't take them seriously."

He was packing his briefcase at the time and pushing his mobile phone into his pocket, hoping he had his hotel finder App. He needed to get a boutique hotel or preferably a 5 star spa to stay in rural Wiltshire, because he was damn sure he wasn't battling the M4 traffic late at night after this gig.

"I mean I don't even possess an Indian Guru outfit that would suit the occasion!" James was chuntering under his breath as he headed out of the office.

At least that was the gist of his conversation with the chuckling Jack who was absolutely certain that James was the man for the job.

Chapter 13

The Indigo Group

As they lingered outside the door to the conference room in rural Wiltshire Lyre was eager to chat with Aramantha to see if their plan for the psychiatric assessments had been fruitful. She was aware that they needed to be discreet in their conversations in this particular venue because it really did attract a diverse, sometimes interesting and often annoying bunch of people. "I am hoping to get more ammunition to entertain my wee psychiatrist friend from what we see tonight. Although I do think he is quite a willing pupil, we are having fun, just wish I were 20 years younger, he is really dishy."

"That never stopped you in previous lives dear friend, but perhaps this life is for other things Mmm?" offered Lyre as Georgina grinned, pretending not to listen whilst her eyes scanned the old portraits along the walls.

"I wonder how many of the luvvy clicks will be here tonight." Mused Aramantha, skilfully changing the subject, as she released Georgina's arm to accompany Lyre. The three women formed into what would soon become a formidable group at the end of the portrait lined hallway. They were about to enter the elegant conference room that had been a dining room in days gone by. The early Chippendale chairs were carefully roped off to one side of the room underneath the enormous gilt framed mirrors and candelabra bedecked side tables. They were met by the sight of a rather sparsely populated circle of velvet covered chairs. Lyre estimated that there were perhaps 40 seats awaiting an audience with only half of the chairs in use. Some eager faces looked up to greet the trio of females as they entered, others were deep in conversation in groups of 3 or 4 standing around the periphery of the circle.

"Ach Gawd!" whispered Az, accentuating her Scottish accent, as she spotted the group leader for the evening, dressed in a long black velvet cloak. His neck was decorated with a long silver chain ending in an enormous quartz orb.

"I see Harry Potter's Voldemort is here again. I wonder where he put the witch's hat?"

"Shush, Az, or we'll be in trouble again for being disrespectful to his *lord ship*."

"Well I mean, just what does he think he is at? If you were to see him working in his bank job in Swindon you'd think he wouldn't say boo to a goose and now look at that."

"Is he a bank manager?" inquired Georgina, finding her voice at last after listening to the chat of the two friends for some time.

"Manager? Not at all he's the lowliest of clerks and he wears those hand knitted waistcoats under his blazer with its threadbare elbows. But here he can take back some power that neither his wife nor his employers allow him in his daily life." Lyre explained.

"I've always thought that he watches too many of those weird cult movies where they always sacrifice the virgins." This was added by Az as all three of them giggled. "He wishes!"

So it was that they entered with smiles on their faces and aroused some interest in the group as to what the joke was. A short, chubby, middle aged man sauntered across to them to give everyone a hug and introduced himself to Georgina. He smelt of lavender and was dressed like a country squire even to the extent of an old fashioned silk cravat tied into his open neck shirt. Georgina was fascinated by someone who dressed like the actor, John Mills, from an old black and white movie. In fact she was starting to wonder whether he was a spiritual energy rather than a living human being until he spoke in a deep baritone voice.

"We are delighted to meet you at last Georgie, my dear, I have heard all about you from Eoin and he reckons there are great things ahead, now you are out and about at last."

"I am flattered, but just what I am supposed to be doing next I really don't know. You make me sound like someone who has just come out of the closet!"

"Nothing to worry about there old girl, all will become clear, don't you worry at all. Sit back and enjoy the ride, that's what I would do. Mind you, don't judge us all by the crowd here tonight, we have some of the luvvies in and they can become a bit annoying."

"I think you mean cloying, Charles don't you?"

"Yes Lyre, you are right there, they do get carried away with their self aggrandisement, not to mention the way they are all so saccharine sweet to each other whilst here and then get the knives out when away from their so called friends and colleagues. They may, of course, be Ok because the knives are silver with crystal handles." Here he stopped to have a chuckle to himself as he visualised what he had said in a farcical way. "I know that some of them are doing good work and raising the vibrations, it's just that sometimes I think they forget that we are all supposed to be working for the light. If we can't work cooperatively together, with light, whilst we raise vibrations, then there will be a problem."

He turned to address Georgina with his final comment.

"I love the way these girls deal with them. They really do have the luvvy bunch wondering what they're up to and whether they should be interviewing them a bit more, just in case they're missing something."

"If only they realised the really boring lives we lead they would not worry so much." Replied Lyre.

"Well yes, that is me, but you certainly don't Lyre, weren't you in Washington last week?" put in Az. "I mean I don't call that boring and I do know that you help hundreds, if not thousands of people every year who in turn raise even more positive energies in their own areas. Oh, *and* she did a spot on Oprah you know Georgie?"

Lyre gave her friend a warm hug as she said; "You are a slightly biased, methinks. It was only because my pal in Chicago knew Oprah and we just got chatting. Anyway, there is no reason why you can't accompany me on some of these trips now that Isabelle is almost a grown woman. But to go back to the 'luvvies' and their problem with us. It really is because we are so open they think we must be hiding something. You know Georgina our motto is always that co operation works more powerfully to raise a light in this world than competition. When we all work together we get the job done more quickly. Cooperation rules supreme but so many in today's society, not just the spooky bunch, want to build their own little sand castles that they never get them done. Unfortunately they also enjoy jumping on other people's without ever seeing that if we all helped with one castle it would be more efficient. You know, rather like the people who lived in small communities used to help each other to build their houses and then move onto the next one."

Aramantha scoffed "Hah, that cant work these days with so much competition to see who has the biggest and the best of whatever money can buy and so many of these people are chasing the same penny. If they shared more they would all also earn more money collectively!" She held her hands outwards to emphasise her exasperation and the abundance that could be received.

At this Lyre turned once more to give Az a hug, changing the subject "I can't tell you how delighted I am that you have been let out tonight and do hope it is the start of you getting back to our old team."

"I think there is more work to do on the family before that happens. Who knows maybe the handsome Dr Jordan will work his magic on them and me. He's talking about family therapy now for goodness sake. Whatever next?" Aramantha turned to scan the room as she spoke. "I see that little witch Juanita here again I am not sure what she gets out of these meetings apart from business cards poached from the rest of us so that she can try to seduce clients from the real clairvoyants and healers. Anyway as for the luvvies I reckon that we should stick to our old friend Eilish's well respected philosophy, you know - send them love and light and fuck 'em! I just love it."

As they exploded in laughter there was a delicate ringing noise made by the small Tibetan bells, firmly held by the bank clerk, come master of ceremonies, calling the group to order. As the friends took their seats they could see that the circle of chairs was now full and some new faces were apparent.

The black robe, rose to greet everyone, acknowledging the newcomers as he did so. He had already had a brief chat with those he did not recognise as they entered the room. His somewhat reedy voice became as deep as he could go and he said

"We have a guest from the media here to observe tonight but he has promised to respect our confidentiality as we request from all visitors. You all know the rules, whatever is mentioned here stays here unless with express permission of the individual who is sharing information with us.

A few hands of dissension were raised at the idea of a media person being present.

"You know we don't approve of uninformed media bods being here unless a vote is taken," spoken by a purple velvet woman, complete with headband. "The last time we were ridiculed in a totally biased un researched Guardian article, it's just not on you know?"

"Now, now James is very respected in the BBC and he is hoping to do a serious programme in the future that will present a balanced discussion around esoteric matters. He has promised not to use anything he sees here without further meetings and research information from as many of you who would like to contribute." The quartz orb was being well squeezed for strength and patience by the group leader as he attempted to placate the dissenters.

James was nodding earnestly in what he hoped was a reassuring manner. "I have made a solemn promise that nothing will be disclosed without everyone's approval. I am a man of my word. I will leave my cards for you to get in contact and discuss whatever concerns you may have."

The whispering buzz circulated as various comments were made, the loudest from another middle aged man in a purple dicky bow. "He'll be the first honourable reporter that I've met in a few years if that is the case!"

A few good humoured laughs and less friendly "harrumphs" resounded from the suitably calmed group. Charles roused himself to say "oh, come on guys let's just get on, young James here will be so impressed with our high connections that he won't dare interfere with the cosmic energies that he will attract into his life after tonight."

James started to rub a hand around his collar and took quite a deep swallow, perhaps of relief mixed with trepidation for what he was going to see. He was really wondering just what he had been coerced into as he smiled rather wanly at the 39 seated individuals around him.

"OK if we are all happy and ready to ascend let's go dear colleagues of the light." Black robe let go of his crystal orb and waved towards the corner of the room.

Now, if you could just start the meditation music Elvira please."

The silver haired Elvira obliged by setting some gentle music recorded from tibetan bowls in motion.

"Breathe deeply and just relax my friends because now, there are words to speak, energies to feel, actions to take, as we seek to put away our thoughts and words in our quest to just *be* … in the now … right now." There was a slight cough from one of the newcomers before he continued; "I know that you can all ground, centre and protect your energy field by now. Put down your roots into the centre of the earth's energy field, visualise your protective shield to encompass this whole room, know that you are safe and I will just pause to invite the angelic realms and energies, from beyond, into our group. We are contacting a divine, intelligent energy this evening, you know how, by activating our hearts and imaginations, our feelings will follow where we need to be. Our expanding electromagnetic field will help in the beginning, getting in touch with the immediate environment, breathe deeply and we can expand our own auras to infinity and beyond … "

With those words everyone present had already closed their eyes, although there was another cough that could have been a scoffing sound, by this time very few were paying any attention to the room. Many had gone inside themselves; others had floated almost immediately into what could be called a variety of out of body experiential states (OBE).

Only James Marwon was peeking through his half closed eye lids, his attention had been particularly caught by an attractive blond haired girl on the other side of the circle. She looked fresh faced, a nose dusted with freckles, lightly tanned and very natural with her long shiny hair and open smile. Her smile seemed to light the room when she had been chatting with two older women and the portly old guy from a black and white movie. He was slightly disconcerted to see another woman viewing him out of one eye as she too scanned the room checking what may be happening around her. Her darkly kohled eyes and gypsy dress style labelled her as a South American if not a Spanish Flamenco dancer. He was wondering what they were all doing as they appeared to relax and almost sleep on their uncomfortable chairs. He almost envied the peaceful auras around him.

Georgina re focussed in her meditation to find that the room around her had changed very quickly into a crystalline structure like a dome of pure white quartz, shining and reflecting rainbows into the circle, on second glance she discovered it was actually a cone shaped structure like an Indian tipi but reaching high into the sky allowing a light like very bright sunshine to flow through in a prismatic way allowing the rainbows to dance around. The ornate ceiling and roof had just seemingly disappeared from her reality and this energy filled atmosphere welcomed her with tingling all around her body. She took a deep breath to really just *be*, as instructed. Her eyes went immediately to the other side of the circle to a familiar face that she had not previously noticed. She gasped "Thomas!" Her need to run to him was pre-empted when she realised that she could float over to give him a hug without physically leaving her chair. She had not seen him in over 10 years, her feelings of love and great friendship were as if they had never been parted. Her energy field floated out of her physical body as though it were something that she did every day and they met somewhere in the middle of the circle.

"How come I didn't see you when I sat down, you wonderful man, you?"

"Hello my beauty, well that would have been because I wasn't there. Actually neither are you right now but I am very pleased that you can see me again tonight, it's been a long time eh?"

Georgina was just gaping at the apparition in front of her and grinning in that happy love struck way, until she realised that she was supposed to answer this old friend.

"Indeed it has and I owe you so much, so much you'll never know. You were my private educator really, and also my listening post and my balance about all things. I am so sad that we lost touch. I know it is almost inevitable when people go off to University, but I never did know where you went?"

"You mean you really don't know?"

A thought hit her like a gong, of course why hadn't she realised before?

"After Eoin's visit I guess I should have realised, but you will remember how I spent a lot of time denying my gift, if that is what it is called. I really did regard you as my pal and I never felt frightened when you were with me from such an early age, I felt that we even started school together. Retrospectively I see just how much denial I have practised in my 33years."

"We all do that, but yes, I was with you from birth (probably slightly before actually). I remember trying to call you down the birth canal as you were a bit reluctant to take over this body and I had to remind you that you had in fact elected to do this trip."

"So no one else ever saw you all that time that we had such wonderful conversations, not even my brothers?"

"You got it Georgie, I was your spirit guide for the first 17 years of your life, then you were just sort of left to get on with it as you were in that academic mode that gives protection from sensitive spiritual feelings for a lot of the time. You had to listen to all those old assumptions being made by the science and philosophy tutors in order to know how so called experts have sat upon scientific and spiritual development with their dogmatic, materialistic views. Mind you I did hear that you were at your work anyway, with a few spirit guides finding you very useful in their spare days."

"Yes I did indeed do some *work* as you call it, just because so many people needed a helping hand – or should I say a helping spirit now?" Thomas nodded and smiled at her open, pretty face.

"I always worried in case I should not be dabbling, mostly I think, because when I went to that spiritual church in my home town they made me feel unworthy in some way, I doubted my abilities when I was with them even though I could see spirit and met some very good people there. If it hadn't been for good old Bronwen I would have cracked up long ago."

His energy field expanded to give her a cosmic hug. A warm loving glow that reassured her beautifully, even without words.

"You were always too kind Georgie. I am so glad that they didn't get you to conform to a rigid template of clairvoyant psychic practise. You are so much bigger than that. Speaking of which have you published your thesis yet?"

"How come everyone is so interested in my academic work, in fact how come you all know about … no, silly question I know that now."

She had in fact given the manuscript to a publisher and it was about to be launched within a few weeks. She had no idea what that really meant, having been delighted that someone was willing to put her words into print. It was with a small publishing company who specialised in academic works. In fact there had been a message on her answer machine as she was leaving home today asking her to call Maurice at the publishers urgently.

For now she was just happy to snuggle into the loving energy field that was her old friend, amazed at how she had never understood that no one else in her family had ever known that he was there. No wonder she had never felt lonely, nor had she needed that continual reassurance that many of her girl friends needed in the form of groping adolescent boys or acne laden cheeks caressing her neck. She had always felt loved and safe in her own company, not realising that her soul was being nourished by universal knowledge and energy from another dimension. On hindsight she could only compare that self possession with that of her devoutly religious friends, although they always seemed fearful about doing something wrong and upsetting their church or family. What a lucky, charmed life she had lead up to now and how grateful she really was. She couldn't wait to share all this with Kyrie and Bronwen. What a shock they would get. Come to think of it how come she had never really discussed Thomas with Bronwen? After all it was her who had moved him from his seat that first day in school. Weirder and weirder, she thought.

As she sighed deeply in reflection, Thomas nodded and agreed with her thoughts, without saying a word. His inherent ability to enter her mind and total energy field without effort was wonderful for her. He was back, how wonderful was that for her new life about to begin?

"You had better get back into your body lovely lady or we may be joined out here by a few more unwanted energies any minute now. There are some, shall we say, different energy forms here tonight. I think that you will soon see that there is a particular group of Indigos with things to do, oh hello, wise one."

An even larger energy field zoomed into view behind Georgina and she felt yet more loving tingles envelop her as a light filled body floated beside Thomas.

"Hi Chaps, I am so pleased that we are all together again at last." Eoin's velvety tones embraced them both. Georgina couldn't help but think of how they must have looked to anyone lucky enough to observe this meeting somewhere in the ether above the group. She giggled to herself that perhaps they looked like three large versions of Casper, the little ghost from the film. She only hoped that there were non of those green slimy, bad spirits around too.

"Oh they are around in different forms but nothing to worry bout with your powerful light shining dear girl." Eoin had already entered her energy field and read her thoughts perfectly with no words needed. "Now you must remember to ring Maurice at the publishers as soon as you get home young woman!" Was there no one who wasn't interested in her bloody thesis? She smiled at Eoin who appeared to be in a white cotton Indian gurus outfit tonight as he swirled about in the ether.

"I promise I will because I'm beginning to see that there is something important going on here that I can be a part of very soon, can't I?"

"Indeed you already are, my dear, in fact that is exactly what you were reincarnated to do."

"Really? Then why did it take me so long to remember my background and life mission?"

"Not everyone needs to retain direct memory in their DNA, consciousness expands the DNA within the human system and we are allowed to take our own time from birth, depending on how we have been pre coded. When in the other dimensions we see so much information that is still in infancy here in earth school. I do know, though, that living humans are not victims of their genes each individual is a master of there own life. Wonder what happened to that Human Genome Project that was looking at DNA."

Here Eoin stopped to shrug his shoulders, the action looking rather odd in a non physical energy field. The rays of energy that radiated and sparked from his light looked a bit like a wet dog shedding water droplets as he shook.

"It is apparent that babies are being born every day now with a higher level of consciousness that supports a higher level of DNA function. I'm really not sure what the boffins on that project made of this information if indeed they discovered it. Ask Lyre about her clients and how many anxious parents come to her with over active toddlers who just need to be understood for their inherent knowledge. Some of these new children do know more than adults. ADHD is another of those labels invented by medics as an excuse to dope the wilder active kids into some sort of submission to society's inane rules. The terms Indigo and Crystal children have been used for many years, without anyone really doing research that can be validified, unfortunately. Of course some parents just have badly brought up little brats and they would love a nice convenient label like this!"

Eoin's chuckles floated around the trio like an orchestra of happiness.

"I know that during my own thesis research I looked at the traditional theorists like, Freud, Jung, Maslow, Piaget, Skinner and the like but no one really seemed to be able to answer or even address the problems surrounding children with special gifts in an acceptable way for me."

"Well exactly, because you *were* one of those children, probably an Indigo before your time." Added Thomas with pride glowing from his eyes. "This is partly why we call our group the Indigo 33, although I prefer to see it just as us 5 with a few angels on the periphery waiting to help, what do you say Eoin?"

"Actually Thomas I think she is more likely to be a diamond classification, that is if I approved and I don't, of these framed boxes, categories, which earth based society insists on giving to its people. Pigeonholed, I think is today's expression that I find particularly vulgar and so unnecessary!"

Georgina was happy to join in here "Yes I agree I think that so many people lose their individuality by being framed and shoved into a small confining, pigeonhole by the people around them, especially families who love to put a label on their siblings before they know who they are."

She was encouraged by the heightened vibrations lightening Thomas and Eoin's energy fields.

"I came across some work called Identity Structure Analysis (ISA) during my thesis and it shows quite clearly how identity can be skewed by family, social groups and society in general. I would love to have an opportunity to do more research with special children."

"Sorry Georgie, you will not have time. There is too much other stuff to do with the facts that we have already, without more expensive research. Every minute is now needed to raise public consciousness before the human race destroys millions of years of hard work by the other dimensions. Thousands of books have been written telling the world how to raise energetic levels to protect immune systems, keep chemical drugs to a minimum, develop a higher consciousness, that can heal both humans and protect our ecosystems but does anyone listen ?" Thomas was also getting quite aerated in his pronouncements.

"Not exactly true Thomas, there is a growing awareness but of course it is being fought hard by the global fiscal policies. The powers that be invent expressions to instil fear into the populace on an almost daily basis. I mean, did you hear that silly American expression, beware the "fiscal cliff" in case you fall off? The large drug companies also have a vested interest in keeping the respective populations somewhat comatose by selling health services millions of pounds of drugs, some useful, some darn right dangerous, unnecessary and relatively un tested." Eoin was vibrating at a very high level now and heating the energy of the little group to resemble a sparkling cosmic soup. "I cannot get into this anymore now or my soapbox will materialise and disturb the group's light work. Mind you, look over there and you will see someone who has never heard of light work at all."

The three energies morphed into one big ball of light, much to Georgina's delight, she felt so empowered by being included into this very special club of inter dimensional workers. As one form they whizzed over to where Juanita in her statutory jingly earrings and gypsy outfit was craning her neck and squinting to see could she read anyone's business cards where some had been dropped under chairs in the enthusiastic welcome hugs.

"Just blow in her ear Thomas old boy and see can you get any reaction." Georgina laughed at this as Thomas did as he was asked. They all smiled to see Juanita shudder and cross herself, as was her habit. She obviously had not managed to go into a meditative state, even with the combined energy field of so many skilled psychics and mediums in the room.

"What a pity, I'm afraid she is a lost cause." Sighed Eoin.

Their ball of combined energy then zoomed over towards where a very bemused James Marwon was sitting trying to look as though he did this all the time. He too was squinting, through lowered eyelids, trying to look at the room whilst pretending to keep his eyes closed in case anyone was watching him. Eoin couldn't resist the urge to detach from his friends and surround James with his energy. The infiltrator's eyes flew open as he shuddered, wondering where the tingling warmth was coming from all over his body.

"Do you know I think he can 'feel' more than the sexy Juanita, amazing!"

Eoin hovered in front of him for a while checking if there was any possibility that James could actually see his energy field. The look of panic in his eyes illustrated quite clearly that he couldn't. He was flicking at his shoulders and generally trying to shake whatever he felt from his body.

"Such a pity as I have great hopes for this young media man, ah well it will take a bit of time I think. Maybe you can help out here Georgina?"

She smiled shyly and said "I'll see what I can do but I can't imagine someone as high profile as this would have anything to talk to little old me about." Thomas and Eoin jointly groaned to such an extent that she looked worriedly at James to see if he had heard the sound.

"No time for silly modesty masquerading as a lack of confidence my dear, just know that you are an important cog in this wheel of world consciousness and you *will* help others to see that they are too. You can work to raise world vibrations *and* have fun you know. So stop it Ok?"

At this, Eoin wafted his translucent arms and they all floated back to their seats and in Georgina's case into her body. She settled just as the Harry Potter extra started to call the group back into consciousness from their respective astral trips. It was obvious to Georgina that Eoin had paid a visit to Lyre's seat on the way back to his vacant place.

Lyre was beaming in an enigmatic way as she gazed dreamily around the group doing her maternal scan, checking who was back in their physical body and who was having trouble returning to the earth plane.

James Marwon, shuddered and was still wondering what had just happened and why the hi tech digital recorder secreted in his pocket was making strange beeping vibrations.

Chapter 14

Lyre the Therapist

She wiggled in a very adult way for a 12 year old, she felt grown up and sexy, she felt slightly giddy and giggly. He said not to make too much noise, but she knew he loved her and that was all ok. Wasn't it?

They were in her mum's front room, the best room, reserved for Sundays and guests on special days. The fire was crackling happily in the tiny tiled grate. She had been watching the flames leap into beautiful patterns, before Uncle Frank had moved subtly along the sofa beside her. The rest of the family were in the kitchen, preparing the ritual Sunday salad, with big smooth fat lettuce leaves, sliced tomatoes, slices of plasticised pink ham and hard boiled eggs. Posh tea they called it, in contrast to the week day bread and jam with cake or just cheese on toast.

She dare not look at him but just tried to focus on the warm and gooey feeling she was getting all over. He said it was ok and not to worry about the rest of the family as he guided her long fingered childish hand towards his leg. She really thought that they ought to clear up the dominoes as they had promised. She kept looking at dominoes that still lay scattered around the table, near their empty box and thought to herself "who cares about clearing them away, promise or not, this is much more exciting. I don't want this feeling to stop." Until now that game of dominoes had been the most exciting event of the afternoon.

How could something that made her feel so nice be wrong? She knew that she was tall for her years, her long gangly legs made her look like Jayne Mansfield, so he said, legs that were to be her pride and joy until the day she died.

What Uncle Frank was doing gave her feelings that she had never experienced before. But no matter how nice it felt, at the edge of her awareness was a small voice telling her how wrong this was and every time she focused on that voice a feeling of cold dread crawled its way along her intestines like ice climbing up a vine. Her mind was caught between physical ecstasy and mental torture bound in guilt and yet the physical ecstasy seemed to be winning, the guilt could wait as long as uncle Frank did not stop what he was doing to her. She practised snaking one of these legs over his knee now, hiding her hand that was learning how to make this man happy. A man that she had known and trusted since she was born. He was the kind uncle that everyone loved for his charm and empathetic nature. "Such a nice man, so thoughtful and kind!"

Freda slid one of her long slim legs over Frank's aged knee as she gazed up into his face, a face she had loved and worshipped for so many years, his eyes closed a smile of pleasure just touching his lips, everybody loved uncle Frank's charm and empathetic nature. "Such a nice man, so thoughtful and kind." How could anything he helped her to do be wrong? Everyone liked him. So why was this a secret to be kept between them? But she would keep the sordid secret until it curled into her soul. The secret that became buried in her subconscious until she realised that something was eating into her happiness in later years. The secret that would need professional help to allow her to purge her guilt.

How come she felt so guilty and naughty when she was alone in her bedroom? Did he really love her, or was it just words …? Her limited experience of boys had been at the local skating rink when once again her long slender legs were much admired by spotty adolescents who liked to help her up when she slipped onto the icy floor.

Those quick gropes of her knees were nothing compared to this thrilling ecstasy when Frank managed to get her to do anything that he asked for. Her childish body had not cared, she just liked it.

Her more bookish friends could have told her right from wrong, but she didn't read much other than women's magazines, occasionally, when her Mum brought them home from the more worldly auntie's house. They were mostly concerned with chintz curtains or how many weeks a girl should hold hands with her boy friend before the first kiss. There were no explanations for what she felt on those stolen damaging Sunday afternoons.

Lyre leaned forward in her leather chair towards the reclining figure of the 60 year old woman, with an old fashioned blonde perm, who was crying softly on her treatment room couch.

"So Freda, tell me why do you think that you have only just managed to remember all of this now?" Freda had called Lyre on Kyrie's advice, for help with her recurring dreams. One terrifying dream was of a wedding day to a monster like creature that would not go away. The creature was wearing leather breeches and sandals and showing her his home through a wooden framed archway. She knew that she was the bride and that she was supposed to go into the ancient hovel. In her dreams and in a previous regression session, with Lyre, she could smell the damp floor and the wood smoke from the open fire place. She had been surprised at how clearly and quickly she had regressed into the scene that felt so real.

"I don't know, but I suddenly feel there is some connection between the monster like creature of my dreams and uncle Frank from my childhood. It is odd that until you put me into hypnosis I had completely buried that memory. Who would have thought that I could forget something so really bad?"

"Yes it was traumatic for you, but you need to know it was not your fault, you were a child. In all child abuse cases it is the adult who is responsible although many try hard to use a myriad of excuses, including blaming a precocious teenager for a 'come on' attitude."

Lyre, walked across the office to fill a crystal glass with water for Freda. She handed it to her as she continued;

"When we went into past life regression do you remember who that mediaeval looking man was, the one in the leather tunic and a small stone cottage?"

"He was the monster in my dream… but when I think about it, he also looked like uncle Frank in this life."

"Yes I suspected as much, sometimes, and I *do* mean only *sometimes*, child abuse in this life is as a result of un resolved relationships in previous lives. People who had been adults together in a sexual relationship previously can re incarnate out of sequence and feel the subconscious need to re enact certain aspects of an old karma even though it is inappropriate and illegal."

"Oh my God, can it not be controlled then?"

"Yes of course it can, depending upon how evolved the soul is, but very few therapists are aware of this and rarely recognise the root cause. Only yesterday I was with a group of people who were working together in the higher dimensions and we actual discussed this with spiritual energies and the Angelic realms. It was amazing just how many spirit guides have been working to try and prevent this kind of thing happening because it so destructive for a weak or immature soul. The Guardian Angels were stating that even though they are unable to disrupt a person's free will they try their hardest to influence the soul and mind of the would be victimiser and that when the victim called out for their help it could strengthen their influence. But Guardian Angels do say that they are powerless to help unless the earth person asks for their intervention!"

"Gosh, sounds a bit like some social workers down here doesn't it?"

Both women smiled at this as Lyre went on to discuss the potential to ask for help from spirit guides and angels if it felt right for the client's soul journey.

"You know in my first session here with you I could actually feel the energy change in the room as you talked to me. When I got to lie on the couch and just listen to your voice I thought that you were actually touching me but then I realised it wasn't your hands but some other force surrounding me with a tangible glow. So was that an angel or what exactly?"

"It could have been any of what I call the helping energies from a number of different dimensions. The healing force that exists in and around the physical universe. When called upon it manifests into this world to bring help and healing where it is needed. Sometimes it is just that healing energy force that comes by the light or it could have been your own guardian spirit or angel or even a passed over loved one calling by to give you a boost."

"It better hadn't have been that bastard Frank, he did enough touching thank you very much! That shit can stay very dead and not get any more chances at this life."

"I don't think he would come to you again without asking permission to enter your energy field first, sometimes they try a few times to come back to ask for forgiveness or to say they are sorry you know?"

"He can piss off!"

"I know what you mean, but do be aware that when they pass over to the light again they have a life review and I suppose get to see the error of their ways and all that pain that it entails. If the lessons are not learned in this earth school then they sometimes get allocated to a future life where they also suffer and learn the lesson in a different way. I know because I meet those troubled souls in the clinic or healing workshops."

"Now THAT I like, sort of like a cosmic zapping with a bloody great cattle prod eh?"

"Mmm, well maybe not quite like that but you're on the right lines, but you do know that the more we can forgive in our lives, the more likely we are to be able to enjoy better times here and in later lives. Forgiveness is a biggy I know and very difficult to do but I always say it is worth thinking about for your own mental health."

"It's funny because Kyrie, you know Georgie's pal who lived in my old street, that's why I came to you in the first place, well she said something similar to me. Seems like I am getting a wee prod from a few different directions ... "

Here Freda burst into giggles as she reflected upon what she had just said.

"Oh I'm sorry It's just that I was thinking about Kyrie too and of course she is a "*wee prod*," you know a wee protestant girl from Belfast?" She continued chortling at the synchronicity of her thoughts and the signs that were coming to her in obscure ways.

"Do you know when I start to put these things into perspective I can see that there are quite a few ways that past lives could influence how we react and the daft things I worry about in this life that I wondered why."

Lyre always enjoyed working with Freda for her sense of humour and genuinely grounded love of life that shone through all of her anxieties.

"Wondering why is a healthy question many people go through a whole life time without asking any questions about themselves or of themselves you know? I am so pleased that you are starting to put things in order in your own mind."

"I have you and Kyrie to thank for that I suppose, doesn't mean I don't want to kill that shit Frank, though, pity he's already dead!"

Lyre smiled at her client and put her arm around her shoulder as she walked her to the door.

"Yes I know, perhaps we still have a bit of work to do together then, see you next week?"

"Wouldn't miss it, now I'm off to share this with Kyrie she'll be flabbergasted. She's moved to a smart new flat in Tooting so I might just get a cup of tea over there before I head home."

Georgina was waiting in the room outside as Freda sauntered out looking pleased with herself. They hugged as Georgina sent her love to Kyrie.

"You know I have you two girls to thank for getting me along to see this angel of a woman! All that depressing shit I have been holding onto in my head for so long was just doing me no good at all. In fact it was really starting to eat at my body you know? I really was getting physically sick, all aches and pains like, all over. I'm gonna tell that mad idiot Eddie to get along here just in case he goes back to snorting himself to death."

"Don't you worry about him Freda, Georgina has him well in hand. In fact I think he is already beginning to wonder what hit him. A sort of thunderclap of positive energy released into his solar plexus and opened all of his senses in a clear clean way that no drug could compete with. in fact he has been clean for a few months now."

Georgina was blushing and giving her usual coy look of self deprecation at this praise from her older mentor. She hugged the now slightly bemused Freda once more as Freda bounced out of the door way with a cheery "He certainly looked good at the girl's housewarming party, but I'm gonna check him out anyway and see what this solar whatnot looks like! I am so glad that Bronwen and Kyrie got that great flat together, it is so right for them. And it gives me an excuse to go shopping in a different area without telling the old man too much!"

Lyre and Georgie grinned at each other conspiratorially. Freda headed off to the elevator that would take her to the real world outside of this cosy therapeutic nest. Lyre hugged Georgina with real affection and slipped her arm around her shoulders to guide her into the apartment that lead off her consulting rooms. Georgina was wrapped up in a stylish cream trench coat, neatly belted at the waist. Her brown leather boots enhanced her slim legs as she walked beside her friend and inspiration.

"Come in and tell me all dear girl."

"Well that James Marwon wants to do an interview with you and me, what do you make of that!"

"Oh now it starts." Said Lyre with a slightly pensive expression on her face.

Eoin was already zooming in from only he knew where.

Chapter 15

Now it Begins

There was no surprise for either of them as the two women stood respectfully to one side allowing the glowing energy that was Eoin to descend or more accurately materialise into the middle of Lyre's consulting room. He managed to follow them into the apartment without any effort and metamorphosed into the handsome, mature male energy field that he had chosen to be today. Georgina found that she was getting quite used to this phenomena that would have shocked almost everyone that she had known in her old life. She now counted her "old life" as before completing her thesis for her final degree or "before Eoin," in fact she often called it B.E. and then consoled herself with the fact that she was now in the state of being "in the moment" and chuckled to herself when she advised non spiritual friends to just "be"! If only they really knew and understood about all of this real spiritual energy stuff, what a film she could make.

Lyre was standing in the middle of the glowing energy that was Eoin, with a beautiful smile on her face as if he were hugging he all over. Georgina was undecided as to whether she should look away, but they turned to her in unison and included her in a slightly less intense version of a cosmic hug.

"Well, well, we were right then eh?" Eoin's gentle tones emanated from a wonderful light filled body that seemed to be clad, today, in a Victorian smoking jacket with silk cravat and odd little tasseled cap stuck jauntily on his head. Lyre became aware of this outfit as soon as she stepped out of his energy field,

"Oh my goodness, Eoin wherever have you been? Looks like a Dickens novel or some such, just landed, I think we need a glass of wine before we can face chatting with you, well at least Georgie and I can have one, come on."

She linked her arm through Georgina's and led the way into the elegant marble topped kitchen that was all stainless steel appliances encased in richly grained, lime washed wood. Her wine cellar was in her kitchen in the form of a chilled cabinet keeping her prized collection at just the right, year- round, temperature. As she performed an amazingly deft action with another piece of stainless steel kit, a cork popped from a chilled Bourgogne Aligote with a satisfying plop. Georgina now knew her way around the kitchen and produced 2 chilled crystal glasses, from the deep freeze, to receive this nectar from the Gods, or as Eoin insisted on calling it "rats' pee!"

"So our James took the bait then?"

"I'm not sure that I like being called "bait", but he has been charming in a bit of a lounge lizardy way, if you know what I mean"?

"Yes dear we certainly do, it seems to go with intransigence and overconfidence in the male of the species. I see it particularly in the media guys. That does not mean, though, that he can't be trained and/ or seduced by a stronger power." Lyre sighed as she looked towards Eoin's energy where he was sniffing the wine bottle with a decidedly disapproving expression on his face.

"Don't know why you buy this acidic stuff, why not get a decent Pomerol in for sipping with your friends? Don't you remember that delicious 1909 we drank in Bordeaux, when was it now? Must have been 1920 ish?."

"That was a red, I do remember but I'm not sure we need to reminisce about wine from other lives right now Eoin dear, something cosmic is really about to happen, well at least it could be powerful if we pull the energy fields in the right direction, don't you think?"

"You know I'm not really au fait with the media world of today's yuppie set, but I do know that something good is on its way. What say you Georgie? Are you ready for a public debate in front of millions of people on television and the worldwide net?"

"James has asked to interview me about my thesis and also anyone else that I would like to accompany me. So I just knew that it had to be Lyre, she has been so supportive and has more universal, cosmic knowledge with scientific evidence than anyone else I have met, well that is those in an earth bound body of course!"

Eoin was glowing in a sparkly bubble now, floating above the kitchen counter and felt the need to remind them both of the dangers inherent in such public debate; "he will be hell bound on making you look ridiculous, of course, think you're ready for that?"

Georgina tried to hide her blushes as she thought back to the last date, disguised as a planning meeting, that she had had with James. From the lingering looks and tingling skin as they brushed past each other in James' office she knew that this relationship was destined to be much more than business. The drink in the local wine bar afterwards had been particularly difficult because her intuition was telling her that she could trust this media man, although her natural caution was trying to reel back the pheromonal reactions for a later date. She coughed to clear her head before saying; "I know it won't be easy, but I feel confident that my research was well done and the conclusions drawn are well represented in worldwide literature. It's just that the pseudo scientists like to pretend that there is no such thing as written, well recorded evidence for universal energy fields that hold "other" life forms, or a continuing life form after the body dies. You know how they like to repeat all that rubbish about there being no scientific facts and validity in research."

"We know that this thesis is stating very strongly a lot of facts that have previously been sat upon or relegated to whimsy files. I really like the way that you have reinforced the voices of eminent scientists and collated their studies from away back in history. Who was it said *science without religion is lame, religion without science is blind* ? I really liked that." Asked Lyre.

Eoin was delighted to be able to show off his knowledge once more,

"That'll be Einstein of course. Ah yes I remember when he was writing up a lot of his work. Do you know that by the age of twelve, he had taught himself Euclidean Geometry, that was around 1891, I seem to remember."

Georgina continued the theme,

"I didn't know that and I studied some of his papers for my thesis. I just know that like so many of his generation he was ridiculed although he published many papers of central importance to the development of 20ᵗʰ Century physics. It wasn't until his theory that starlight would bend near something like the sun was confirmed during a solar eclipse that he became world renowned and respected by the doubting Thomas's as far as I can see."

"Absolutely!" added Eoin, now on a roll, "That was in 1919, and then he received his Nobel Prize in Physics in 1921, even incredible information does eventually get seen to be believed, so to speak!" He was grinning broadly and floating excitedly above the counter once more. "How I love historical facts, most especially when I was actually there and can remember it happening .... just wish he would have brushed his hair occasionally, that's all."

The two women laughed at Eoin's excitement and irreverence towards such a genius.

"I could have done with you around me in those early research days Eoin, I could just have interviewed you instead of ploughing through the papers. I even looked at Nietzsche and his influence on Jung's work. In fact I started to worry that by even studying all of this I could be labelled as insane as they did to poor old Nietzsche. It certainly is a bit mind bending trying to collate it all and come to conclusions that were well documented and correlated across so many different scientific and religious documents all of those years ago. I often wondered why I was bothering to say it all again!"

Lyre interjected here, "if that were the case no one would have bothered to write anything since the ancient cultures were reported in hieroglyphics or even cuneiform. It has probably all been said before but there are always anomalies and inconsistencies to be discussed to allow free thinking and free will in life decisions."

"Thomas used to say exactly that in our discussions when I was young." Georgina agreed.

"Plus we have to remember that some people are just *thick* don't you know!" Eoin was able to bring the chat back to every day language with no problems at all.

The three friends continued to discuss a strategy for the proposed television interview that was to form part of a programme about the afterlife and spiritual belief systems.

Georgina was focussing on the part of her thesis that had most impressed James Marwon. "James was just flabbergasted that there is so much concrete evidence that the human soul does continue after the body dies. He was particularly fascinated by the studies that I reported showing clearly that some cross gender behaviour in this life has been brought in from an old life where the subject was a different sex."

"Yeeers well, of course, he knows the media love all that stuff that they can put a kinky spin onto my dear, you know lesbian or gay sex that excites them so much. We have to make sure he doesn't focus on something just because it has a sexual connotation, that always messes up a programme and the next day reviews." Eoin's glow was darkening at the memory of how such things had occurred in past publicity.

"But I suppose where the lingering memory of being a different sex before causes a distinct hatred of certain physical features in their present body could be discussed with factual evidence. You know, where this in turn results in illness for their body because of a negative energy field blocking the body's natural flow. It is becoming increasingly recognised, as Georgina so correctly wrote in her thesis, that self hatred can cause physical illness." Lyre was warning to this particular line of discussion.

"That may well come up but I will, of course, be around to help out in case of dilemma as usual, you need to remember these Beeb boys are not as open and aware as the lovely Oprah was the last time, Lyre, eh?"

"Now, now Eoin, you need to be careful. You remember the time we did, or rather, *I* did that radio programme and your energy blew all the computer kit up. What a mess that was for several minutes until they were able to run a secondary system into the studio."

Georgina was giggling to herself as she envisaged the phenomena that was Eoin flying around a television studio blowing lights and cameras as he materialised in and out. She wondered if he would appear in shot like the spiritual orbs that were now making themselves visible on digital photographs.

"I may invite Thomas to come along and keep a helpful energy shield in operation for you too. Yeeeas … (he appeared to be stroking his diaphanous chin as he thought out loud), it would be a good idea to set up some kind of grid around the studio, can't have any of those goblin types popping in to cause havoc."

"Goblins!" Georgina was raising her eyebrows as she sipped the chilled wine.

"Oh yes, little gits have been known to muscle in when we are trying to spread light, they don't mean to do harm really. It's just that they have a remit to provide a sort of cheeky balance, shall we say in earth's society? They tend to forget the definition of 'balance' at times and tip the scales too far into the dark side. I have tried to get them to think more about the yin, yang philosophies in a positive manner but they can get carried away."

As Eoin explained Lyre topped up Georgina's glass and slid some green olives, in a handmade wooden bowl, across the counter towards her young friend. She continued for him.

"I prefer not to talk about them and hence not give any credence to their rather sinister little low vibrations in this earth field. I once had a client who was so tormented that she had been committed to a psychiatric hospital by some twit of a psychiatrist who decided that she was schizoid without any other evidence than that she had reported seeing these nasty little creatures in her bedroom every night." Lyre was getting riled up when she thought about such a common misdiagnosis and went off to find the case file in her office.

Eoin winked at Georgina as he smiled proudly at his great love's passion for her job.

"Yes here it is, she reported three creatures, looking rather like Dobby in Harry Potter films, that poked her and removed the bed covers just as she was dozing off."

"They do actually, or rather they CAN look like that if they chose to!" Here Eoin was nodding enthusiastically and chuckling to himself.

"It certainly wasn't funny for that poor girl. Luckily her family had heard about me and asked that I visit her apartment, and do you know they, the little demons, were still there hoping she would be back soon, as she had been such a novel piece of fun for them. Had I been able to help her earlier she could have learned to deal with them herself. She really is much more sensitive to energies than her family had understood, well why would they really?"

"So what happened how did you get the institution to release her?" Georgina was feeling concerned at such injustice.

"Oh, once I had a couple of sessions with her and she realised that I had actually seen the pesky little creatures too, she knew that there was nothing wrong with her apart from being in a higher vibrational state and having a gift that she could eventually use. She stopped worrying about her own mental state. It is society that often causes specially gifted children to be wrongly labelled. I always advocate looking to the professional doing the labelling first and *then* decide about the child. The rows I have had with educational psychologists!"

Eoin was looking delightfully proud as he nodded with enthusiasm at Georgina to support his love's intelligent ability to solve life problems. "She's not just a pretty face you know!"

Georgina smiled and nodded in agreement.

"Unfortunately, in this case, the psychiatrists were not as happy to accept my consultancy work and we had to do what so many other special people have had to do in the past and just get her to agree that she saw nothing and had been having a personal crisis at the time. She really did have to deny her own truth to appease these narrow professional assessors. It was easier to let them have their initial assessment of 'hysteria' and 'stress' confirmed than to try to educate them about different vibrational states in our world today. They were happy to release her a few days later when she relaxed into a 'normal' state that reassured her doctors that she was not schizoid after all. How I hate that word normal, what does it mean? I won't get onto my hobby horse now but you both know what I mean, toeing a societal line of conforming to what, for God's sake?"

"Never mind the millions being spent on psycho pharmaceuticals, we could fill twenty programmes .... Ah well, let's get down to business then." Eoin pulled their discussion back to the impending

BBC interviews as the women settled onto some stylish high stools at the kitchen counter.

Georgina pulled her I Pad from her bag and prepared to make notes.

"Which aspects of your thesis does your James suggest that he will focus on for starters?"

"He's not *my* James, but I think he's genuinely fascinated by the concept of the eternal energy field or soul energy. I provided a lot of evidence for this by citing so many excellent papers from the scientific fraternity. The added plus of having witnessed so many real time experiments in the States of course made him sit up and take notice more than ever. I may be naive because I really think he wants to believe the evidence he read there, but like so many people he has never been able to experience the energy field for himself. You know he came to that meeting in Wiltshire, hoping to learn, but he came with more than cynicism, he came with a closed personal space that even if Archangel Michael himself had sat on his knee he wouldn't have felt the tingle!" Eoin was smiling now.

"Well I did try to wake him up before he left by interfering with his recorder and the cell phone was all I could activate. His own aura remained, as you say, closed and unresponsive. Mind you he did go away looking …. shall we say … slightly quizzical?"

"Once fear comes into it, of course there is a bigger job to do. Damn nuisance that we have all of these silly, spooky, ghost hunting programmes on the telly right now that give the wrong message - all that screaming and running around in dark dungeons just does no good at all for our cause." Lyre was always trying to educate with her professional presentations, scientifically reported papers and books showing the unifying potential of the greater consciousness.

"I'm not averse to a bit of haunting when the cause is justified you know, but I accept that what we need right now in the quest to raise the earth's vibrational level is level headed common sense in the presentation of facts. Non frightening, verifiable facts at that, where we can help everyone to 'feel' energy and know that they can access it, dead or alive." The deep chuckle emanating from Eoin as he finished this sentence caused the women to look at him for clarification.

"Oh, I was just imagining one of those old cowboy posters - you know, *"Wanted - soul, dead or alive"*, I always think a bit of graphic imagery doesn't go amiss in these situations."

'Perhaps we can suggest a sort of interactive programme where we encourage the audience to 'feel' their own auras."

Georgina was getting into her stride now.

"Ooer ducky! Can you imagine how that would be received? How big is your aura sir? Hah!" Joked Eoin. Although he loved to find the fun in most things, but was very aware of how the media enjoyed twisting innocent statements to ridicule the topic discussed.

Lyre decided it was time to bring the trio to order; "I think that is an excellent idea, after all they did all that Yuri Geller stuff years ago where they illustrated spoon and fork bending across the airwaves and it seemed to grab people's imaginations."

"Yes until the fearful bastards spread word that it was a con and all that other stuff that they like to put out as soon as possible after such successful experiments have shown the power of what they liked to label 'the human mind'. Yuri did great work, noticeably, I think that he was quickly nabbed by some secret Government organisations across the world, who always pretend they don't believe until they *need* a bit of help from the other side. We're talking about changing international views here. This has such a powerful potential, get this right and not only will we attract a lot of opposition, always good for publicity, but also open minds to the most profound human mysteries of generations. I do love a bit of boat rocking. This stuff transcends all religious, scientific and spiritual beliefs from the beginning of time. Wow, even I am getting excited now!"

Eoin appeared to flop down into the black Le Corbusier leather chair that had been tastefully situated in the corner of the kitchen. He looked around at his perching place, "Never understood why these things became so extraordinarily expensive my dears. I remember meeting the young Charles Edouard away back in the twenties. He didn't seem so remarkable then. In fact I wasn't really impressed until I saw that beautiful modern city that he designed in Chandigargh ... mmm India, I do so love the place, pity about the hygiene standards for western immune systems!"

Georgina turned to Lyre with an amused smile that asked so many questions. Her older friend immediately responded with a sigh, rolling her eyes to the ceiling; "I don't know how he does it, rambling off into another life, another era, and now we are into Charles- Edouard Jeannet, wonderful Swiss designer who we knew away back at the beginning of his design career in his thirties. Have to say I too enjoyed some romantic times in Chandigarh, his work there made quite a change. But you know Eoin, I'm not too sure it is relevant to our media discussion right now?"

Eoin responded with "Nice chair though, have to admit, I prefer it to your dining room Ghost chairs from that new chappie Philippe Starck." here another of his chuckles - "although aptly named for us don't you think?"

"Ghost chairs, I don't believe it?" Georgina was starting to think she was losing the plot.

"No it is true, that is what they're called. I have great problems with this spook type terminology, although you have to admit to call something 'ghost' because you can see through it is not exactly rocket science. It does however give me hope that there is a positive aspect to the word ghost, ghost like, spirit energy and the rest. There used to be a group in Canada called 'Spirit in Business' I quite liked that because they made it mainstream to use spiritual energy in a scientific scenario. Many businesses contributed, I do wonder if they are still about. I just never get the chance to pop off and do the research these days."

It was about then that Georgina decided she would have to take control of the discussion again before yet more tangents were explored. She knew that the television programme was an important milestone in her life and really wanted to make sure everyone knew what was happening. She felt very safe knowing that Lyre would be with her as her medical qualifications always lent more credibility to the situation, although Lyre rarely mentioned her academic and medical background. "So would a presenter normally provide guidelines as to what he will ask before we begin the programme?"

"Hah!" Eoin was explosive in his response to this, "Chance would be a fine thing!" Lyre cast a look of warning towards Eoin.

"No, Georgie, they are dead against such helpful preparation in these situations, makes for more controversy and ridicule if they can catch us out, so to speak!"

"Awkward buggers really, never can understand the underlying agenda of these people," Eoin was puffing up again, floating well above the Le Corbusier as he reacted in his predictable manner to the media stereotypes that so irritated him.

"The Problem is they know that if they throw enough mud, some will always stick. Bloody nuisance that it is those little muddy bits that the skeptics love to hone into. It doesn't matter how good the evidence presented, if they want to find a negative aspect they will! I remember on Oprah someone managed to speak out from the audience, when spirits were mentioned - "Ah yes," they said "I do love the spirits myself, whiskey, gin, bourbon and the rest!""

Georgina laughed at this with appreciation. The mention of gin reminded her that she had sipped a pretty strong gin and tonic on her last meeting with James, it had almost led to her responding more enthusiastically to the gentle stroking of his warm hand on her back as they sat in the late evening sunshine outside the London wine bar. She could feel her skin tingling again at the thought. Their thighs had moved closer together under the bistro table and their hands had met on her knee. It was only the discussion of a television show that had kept her grounded and out of the kundalini energy spiral that world have made for a very interesting next step.

Maybe her life would take off in more ways than one after this programme.

Lyre interrupted her daydream ;

"Yes and the place erupted in laughter, that was Ok up to a point, because I laughed too. The problem became that ridicule was then adopted as a method of attack no matter how skilled Oprah was in her supportive questioning. Once the consensus is that you are a figure of fun it takes a lot of control to get back on track and be taken seriously again."

Eoin was floating upwards again as he said; "It was ever thus, because the fearful always pour scorn on what they don't understand. Mockery works to cover lack of knowledge and what's more so many repeat mantras of disbelief that they have forgotten that they can google the research papers now and allow themselves to believe something new. The world is moving so quickly. Speaking of which I had better be off, lots to do, people to see, places to haunt …. Only joking." He added the final word as Lyre raised her eyebrows ceiling-wards once more.

"See you beautiful girls on the night if not before, ciao bellas!"

With this, he continued his upwards float, his outfit morphing into a Venetian gondolier's white trousers and striped top, just as he disappeared somewhere above the wine chiller.

"Obviously flitting off to Italy - ciao bellas - indeed!" Laughed Lyre as she leaned over to study the notes on Georgina's I Pad.

Chapter 16

Chez Aramantha

Aramantha poured one of their finest French merlots as she searched for the TV remote control. Having secured the remote she plumped the cushions on her favourite fireside chair, an overly stuffed, tastefully covered, comfort zone. As she sank into it's depths she checked that the roaring log fire was suitably guarded to protect her colourful Iranian rug from misguided sparks and settled down to watch her good friends on the live show due to broadcast at any moment. It had been a sunny day but the house always benefited from a fire for warmth and ambience.

How long had they all been wanting to do something like this? She knew that it was a powerful moment for the light workers who really cared about not only the world and it's people but the greater energy field that was of Universal importance. How far it would go was another matter. She also knew that she had not been using her ancient knowledge as she would have wished in this reincarnation. It had taken some time to work out quite why she had chosen the life path that had taken her into conflict with several people, not least her husband and now, sadly, even her maturing daughter seemed to be at odds with her mother's beliefs. As she thought about her beloved Izzy, the long legged teenager bounced into the room with a diet coke in her hand. Her long straight hair was flicked silkily over her shoulder as she too found a squidgy comfort zone to snuggle into.

Without forethought Az launched into a well honed mother role, she regularly did this and then mentally kicked herself after speaking.

"Ach Izzy dear surely you're not still drinking that aspartame loaded stuff, it's terrible for you, you're better off drinking real coke."

"Oh, you mean worse than that red stuff you insist on pouring into yourself mother dearest?"

"Well yes, actually it is - at least I know the vineyard that this comes from and I know it is all natural and made from the best grapes with wonderful French sunshine and no added chemicals!"

"Aha but the alcohol content of 13% is doing you no harm then, or was it just the euphoria that had you swaying last weekend as you left the dinner table?"

"Ok sweetie let's call a truce shall we? I just know that I can relax better with a couple of glasses of good wine rather than take the mind altering drugs that our dear Dr Jordan would have liked to prescribe for me. Although I have to say I am warming to that young man. Our discussions have developed amazingly over recent months. Perhaps you would like to come with me some time? I am sure you would like him."

"Yeah, it would be great for my street cred being seen coming out of a shrink's office in full daylight wouldn't it? Anyway what do you talk about that is so fascinating? By the way you started this attack on my 'healthy' drink not me!"

"Ok, fair enough and I think perhaps this programme will shed some light on aspects of my chats with Victor Jordan. Aunt Lyre is being interviewed with Georgina. That rather cute BBC presenter James Marwon has set it up after several months of negotiations with the network. I hope he is kind to them. I think he is getting very interested in Georgie and not just for her PhD research."

"Mmm, impressive, Jimmy the moron, talking about mumbo jumbo, spooky stuff. How did they wangle that? I wouldn't have thought it was up his street. Sounds as though he is taking a bit of a risk with his credibility and ratings. I guess if he thinks it will help him get more cosy with Georgie then he thinks it worth risking the ratings."

"We're about to see, he wouldn't give them any clues about the topics he wanted to cover. Right here we go, lets keep our fingers crossed for the girls."

They both turned to the screen as the opening credits rolled and shots of a studio audience panned into view. Aramantha was dismayed to recognise a few of the audience faces as well known humanist campaigners who loved to argue about anything that they could label as 'spiritual' and try to hang on a religious hook. There was also the media's pet psychologist with a mind so closed it could have been cemented at birth. She was sure that he practised that supercilious, smug smile in front of his bathroom mirror before he shaved. He was making sure that his best intellectually polished cheek, and the topping of quizzically raised eyebrow was being presented to camera as it panned the room.

The usual mixture of television audience participants from the friends of staff to those who had booked their live show tickets months in advance were shuffling in their seats to get the best view of the stage whilst subtly checking where the nearest camera was to their position. She spotted Georgina's Irish friend Kyrie seated between her gay pals sartorial Giles and cheeky Ralph. She wondered whether Freda had managed to get a seat as she had been very keen to participate. Lyre had told Az that her client and Kyrie's neighbour had been raring to get into the open question session at the end of the show so that she could "tell them a thing or two that would rock their boats!" They were all amazed at how much she had gained from past life regression sessions with Lyre. She had even written to a local magazine to let them know how beneficial her new knowledge of past lives had been for, not just her psychological well being, but also her physical health. Freda had really blossomed since her first sessions with Lyre and wanted the world to know about it.

Aramantha was just musing about this success when Karl burst into the sitting room and switched off the TV to shouts of dismay from both his wife and daughter.

"Whatever are you doing Karl? We're about to watch Lyre and Georgina on live with James Marwon!"

"Yes well, that waffle will just have to wait as I have some policemen at the door looking for Isabelle."

The two women gasped as they sprang out of their chairs towards the door. Az, carefully positioned her wine glass on to the side table as Izzy's coke can hit the hearth with a crash.

"Oh shit, sorry Mum it slipped."

The shock of hearing her rebellious daughter say "sorry" was almost as surprising as the fact that there was a detective Inspector at the door with a uniformed constable from the local police station. Her mind was starting to analyse this as Karl went back to the hall to guide the two men into the sitting room. Inspector Martin was tall with pepper and salt hair that seemed to have a mind of it's own, springing up in wiry tufts that he pushed down as he entered the room. He was wearing a well cut grey business suit and a rather snazzy silk tie that appeared to reflect the shine in his deep green eyes. He held his mouth in a controlled line of sufficient seriousness to suggest that he did not like what he was about to say.

"Sorry Mr and Mrs Raven but we really do need to ask your daughter a few questions about where she was last Saturday evening. This is Constable Glass from your local police and I am from Reading C.I.D. I'm Detective Inspector Martin. We are interviewing everyone who attended a party in Reading at …." He flipped open his notebook to check the address that he needed. Karl interrupted immediately with his professional, client pleasing voice.

"Go right ahead, Inspector, I drove her myself to one of her friends' houses on the outskirts of Reading, right Izzy?"

"Err, yes I went to a party with my school friends in Jake's house on the London Road. Is there something wrong with Jake? There was no trouble at the party, that night."

"That night miss? Does that mean there was some trouble on another night then?"

"Oh no, I just meant there was no trouble, because sometimes we have been at parties where there have been gate crashers causing bother. You know how groups tell gangs where to go on Face Book or Twitter and then the whole world turn up when a big party has been announced without permission! We all live in dread of that happening."

"I can imagine, ruddy Face Book. No, we are just making enquiries about a man called Eddie Gethin, ex Welsh Guardsman, do you know him? I believe that he was at that same party?"

"I don't recognise the name. He could've been one of the older group who were there, I suppose, we tend to stick with our school friends because some of the older guys think it's funny to hit on us because we're still at school. I guess they think we're a bit posh when they hear where we live."

"This young man was in his late 30s, miss and would have had a Welsh accent, probably."

At this point Karl interjected,

"Was, Inspector? Is that past tense? Has something happened to him then?"

Izzy was starting to look uncomfortable and perched herself on to the arm of the chair that she had recently vacated. Her mother moved across to put an arm around her shoulders for support.

"He has been found dead of a suspected drugs overdose, Sir, and we have reason to believe that he would have secured himself some extras at that party. It seems to have been his last social outing before death. We need to know if there was enough to kill himself with and if your daughter or her friends saw drugs being used there in serious quantities. We're moving quickly in liaison with our Bromley colleagues in drug squad. It is serious stuff right now."

Az looked across at Karl with raised eyebrows and a shrug of her shoulders that could have meant "told you so" or just a concerned maternal acknowledgement of her daughter's plight.

"When exactly did he do it Inspector?" Karl was feeling the need to escape his wife's eyes as he asked the question.

"I'm afraid I can't really discuss that at the moment sir."

"Isabelle, you do not need to incriminate yourself here by admitting anything that is illegal without my lawyer present you know, that right Inspector?"

Before Inspector Martin could reply, Izzy shook her head and said ; "Mum, dad, I have always told you that I do not dabble and that is perfectly true, so I don't see why I would need a lawyer right now. I can honestly say that I have never tried what my mum calls' mind altering drugs' apart from one horrid quick puff on a spliff when I was about 14, I know, I know," As both parents started to interrupt at once, "but really I hated the taste and the smell so I knew there would never be a repeat performance right there and then." She then added a statement that was music to Aramantha's ears.

"Anyway I can get out of my head any time I like by using meditation. I never told you Mum but I have always used those quiet times, like when I was small and we sat together in a peaceful state. It still helps me."

"I am very pleased to hear that miss, sorry to come back to the party, but you did see others using that night did you?"

"Yes there are always a few idiots who like to look cool and they try whatever is on offer." Aramantha was not really listening now as her soul was quietly singing *she still remembers, thank you, thank you.*

"What exactly was on offer?" Inspector Martin needed his information.

"Oh I really couldn't be sure because it's well known that I just don't go there, so anyone with gear on them keeps it out of my way. If anyone's doing lines or shooting up they do it in the loo, so again, unless I really need to go, I stay clear. The music was really good that night and I love to dance, so that's it, I dance."

She glanced across at the younger, good looking Constable who was raising his eyebrows in a rather disbelieving manner as he took his notes.

"I'm not a boring goody goody you know, I just know that I like being in control of my own mind and for that reason I see no reason to take drugs, or even booze. I can have fun on the atmosphere and the music without all that shit. I am slowly getting more into meditation again to keep calm when I study too."

The Inspector replied quickly, "now, I don't think anyone would consider an intelligent, good looking young lady like yourself to be boring miss. I do know that the media would have us all believe that there isn't a teenager alive who doesn't spend their weekends out of their heads on something or other, but as the father of 3 teenagers myself I know it is wide of the mark. Incidentally they're not boring either and know how to enjoy themselves, a bit too much sometimes I can tell you ..." Here the Constable coughed pointedly, "Anyway that's another story."

"I am just wondering if there is anyone you may be able to recognise from that 'older group' if we were to show you some photographs. No pressure, of course, but it could be very useful to our enquiries to check if this Eddie had any regular scoring partners. Forensics are working on what he had in his system when he died so knowing that and who he was with socially could lead us to a supplier."

Izzy glanced towards her parents who both nodded enthusiastically for her to help out in what was beginning to sound like a serious case.

Eddie's name was also starting to ring bells with Aramantha as she vaguely remembered Georgina mentioning some soul healing work that she had been doing with an ex boyfriend of Kyrie. Surely too much of a coincidence? At this thought her mind wandered back to the television programme that she was missing. She just hoped that it was going well

Chapter 17

Under the Lights

"Now for fuck sake don't go soft on me Jimmy boy, we do need this programme spicy and we need you in Rottweiler mode if we're gonna get the ratings. Let *them* mention spooky stuff, not you. Your job is to look supremely intelligent and rip 'em to bits, verbally of course."

James was in his dressing room with Jack his producer and the weekly programme editor. The pre show briefing was always tight and to the point. Notes and ideas had been flying between them and the research team all week. It had just been nudged into controversy when James mentioned that he would be reporting how the meeting in the Wiltshire stately home had left him feeling.

The fact that his tape recorder had switched off, and it had also managed to record some weird high pitched noises before doing so, had freaked him out more than a little. He didn't mention all of the rather cosy meetings that he had enjoyed with the cute Georgina, off the record, either. Jack, who was no fool when it came to testosterone, had started to wonder just how those few "research" meetings that he did know about finished up. Right now he was beginning to worry that some previously undeclared fringe benefits may be starting to bias his top dog, tough presenter.

"Don't you worry Jack this is gonna be a really fascinating programme. There is just something about both of these women that is incredibly fascinating in a weird way. It'll be good viewing."

"Yeah, well I've got our *friendly* humanist society members well placed to stir things up a bit, not to mention Fritz, the cynic, Keister!"

"Do you really think that was necessary Jack? I mean there is enough genuine skepticism out there without importing any more, surely. It gets boring listening to that twit Keister spouting the same rhetoric about lack of scientific proof, ad nauseum."

"It's done now and all controversy is welcome for the ratings, we have to remember not everyone has seen him wheeled out as the resident anti-spook on every other slightly esoteric show in the U.K!"

Editor, Phoebe, decided it was time to hit the set and coughed strategically to break up the discussion.

"Ok guys let's go get this show on the road. Do you want to walk along to the green room with me Jimmy and we can pick up the ladies?"

"Now there's something he can do with no problem." chuckled Jack as he wandered to the dressing room door. "Lead the way Phoebs, lets move."

James entered the green room to find his guests sitting with their eyes closed and happy smiles on their faces. Was it a coincidence that he felt a prickling sensation in his scalp as he walked closer to their positions on the comfy sofa? He actually shivered as he shook his head to clear the tingling from his scalp. There was a definite warm glow in the room that hosted so many of the guests from one show or another in a busy week. Phoebe, following closely on his heels, stopped too and did a little shuffle with her feet.

"Wow, what's happening here?"

James ignored her and laid his hand gently on Lyre's shoulder.

"Sorry ladies, it's time to go now, hope I'm not interrupting."

Lyre opened her eyes with a dreamy look and immediately flicked into business mode.

"Hello James my dear, we were just meditating to get into the mood, so to speak. We're as ready as we'll ever be, right Georgie?"

Georgina also did that dreamy (and James thought, very sexy) expression as she too came back into her body and, consequently the room, ready to take on the media world for her first broadcast. Her smile to James did wonderful things to his body as he offered her is arm.

"Lead on Macduff!" She linked her arm through James's as she stood, much to the amusement of Phoebe who offered her arm mockingly to Lyre to follow her presenter out of the room.

They were guided along the corridors bedecked with the photographs of programme stars, now known as celebrities, no matter their level of fame or talent. This mixed bunch of celebs gazed at the group as they walked briskly towards the studio. It amused Georgie to imagine each celebrity commenting and changing position, Harry Potter like, as the little group passed, trapped as they were in their static frames. Eoin's voice came very clearly into her head as she was trying to suppress her smiles.

"Stop that, young lady, or you will get a fit of the giggles on the show!"

She looked up expectantly and Lyre too nodded agreeably in her direction as though acknowledging their mutual spirit friend, who had obviously turned up in good time to make his presence known. The air tingled although they couldn't yet see him. It was interesting for the women to watch both James and Phoebe shudder slightly as Eoin's energy passed over their heads.

The studio stage was laid out in the usual chat show style, a night-time panorama of London forming a huge backdrop as though from a window. The presenter's desk was given pride of place noticeably higher than the guests' sofa that was placed at an angle to and considerably lower than the desk. Lyre's shrewd mind instantly saw that it was all designed to put the guest at a disadvantage in the hierarchy of interview techniques. Psychologically the host must remain higher and hence, in control, even more so when the topic was somewhat contentious.

Lyre and Georgina took their places on the soft leather sofa as James slid expertly into his high swivel chair behind the chrome and leather desk. He smiled reassuringly at the two women who he was definitely starting to regard with much more respect than his producer had wanted when initially planning this show.

It was somewhat disconcerting for Georgina to catch sight of Eoin draped in a relaxing style over the far corner of the desk. His outfit of choice for tonight was a white raincoat with turned up collar, over a snazzy suit and a jauntily placed trilby reminiscent of an old fashioned, Fleet street hack. She supposed this was his idea of a suitable media outfit and nodded subtly towards him as he beamed across the desk at her. His glow added to the already rather warm studio lights. She was glad that she had taken Lyre's advice to wear a loose silk shift allowing her lightly tanned legs to stay bare and cool in strappy high heeled sandals. Her silky blond hair floated gracefully over her shoulders in an angelic way.

Lyre, black and white hair carefully coiffed and shining was in her favourite Issey Miyake outfit and looked her usual sophisticated self as she crossed her, still slender, long legs at the ankles, resting her Jimmy Choos gently together. The stylish look of the two women was not lost on James Marwon, well known for the succession of glamorous females that he escorted about town. He was wondering if he could coerce Georgina into going with him to Groucho's after the show, even with Lyre, if necessary. He didn't like to admit that this mysteriously cool blonde had started to get to him in more ways than one. He knew that he could feel her beginning to respond to him in a much more intimate way than he had ever been hoping for. For reasons previously unknown in his courtship rituals he had taken it all very slowly with much more subtle respect than he had paid to previous girls, unless of course they had been the older women who had benefitted his career. He was slowly becoming aware that he was excited on more levels than his basic instincts, about a woman, for the first time in several years. The level of his mind, above his Calvin Klein's, was wondering whether everything could become weirdly over the top during the show. He really was not certain which way the chat would go tonight and for the first time his consummate professional aura was also feeling slightly wobbly.

Deep breath, eyes away from Georgie's smooth tanned legs and her pert little boobs as they pushed against that silky dress and he forced himself to listen to Phoebe in his ear piece, counting them into the show. Lyre was glancing casually around at the audience and nudged Georgina as she saw her friends Kyrie, Ralph and Giles in the studio audience. The new neighbour, Guy the BFBS radio presenter was also there sitting beside a very excited looking Freda who couldn't believe her luck to be in such an exciting venue. James had given some complimentary tickets to both women but it was only Georgina's friends who had made it into the Television Centre.

Aramantha had, of course, decided it would be better to watch from the comfort of home, hoping that Karl would be late at the office to allow her to watch without any scornful comments. Lyre would be really surprised if she had known that her old friend was already involved in those unexpected interviews with the policemen whilst the audience were settling into their seats in London's television centre. Lyre was always comforted by the presence of her very best inter dimensional friend and erstwhile lover in the form or rather form*less* shape of Eoin. She had chosen to ignore his "media hack's" getup for the evening. She also knew that Thomas was lurking somewhere in the rafters of the studio, holding the energy in safety as suggested at their last meeting. The other, highly charged, angelic presence was obvious to both her and Georgina's sensitive energy fields and that comfortable aura filled the studio much to their combined relief.

"Deep breath and relax." Lyre whispered to Georgina.

Once the show went live the energy in the whole studio went live too. The vibrational levels were much more than the studio crew realised as the cosmic energy that was focussing on this small area of London was bigger than an atomic explosion. Every angelic and spiritual presence in a massive radius above and around the area knew that "something big was going down" tonight. This was "Eoin speak" of course, he had watched too many films in his earthbound life. His angel pals thought "going up" would have been a better description of this public discussion about their favourite soul expanding topics, but didn't like to spoil the flow of excitement that Eoin was taking pleasure in orchestrating from his invisible position on the presenter's desk. James skilfully presented the topic by giving a brief synopsis of Georgina's PhD thesis with the title that had caused quite a stir in academic circles when first submitted for assessment, *Angels and Energies in the 21st Century*. The fact that she had been constantly in conflict with her academic supervisors had already prepared her for controversy when it became public. Indeed James introduced it as "The academic thesis that has rocked the theologian and scientific worlds!"

As he announced the title the backdrop of London morphed into the recently published book cover. There it was, for the world to see, a mixture of spiritual orbs in diaphanous colours radiating across a hazy background that intermingled with the title and her name. It seemed to be radiating energy to mix with the electric atmosphere in the room.

Georgina felt her stomach tighten as she heard these words about her work going out to millions of viewers around the world. She knew that the five minute meditation and relaxation space she had shared with Lyre in the green room had prepared her mentally for what was to come but even so the physical reality was so much more than she had visualised. She was confident that she had validified all of her statements and presentations with scientific papers from a worldwide database of research. Even the thesis cover had an incredible story to accompany it. It had appeared one morning on to her mobile phone screen without any interference from her.

Her own original written research had also used credible clairvoyants, energy healers and medically qualified assessors. She had visited many paranormal, psychiatric and parapsychology research centres in Europe, Japan and the United States. A Christmas gift from her loving but somewhat bemused family had been an air ticket to visit some of the top names in psychic research in America. Her Skype calls to centres for excellence in Russia and China had provided many personal interviews with eminent scientists who had been quietly and discretely studying where science had been meeting spiritual/philosophical matter for much longer than the modern media realised or at least admitted. She knew that energy was real, she had seen angels herself in energetic form and she had also seen auras that had been depicted in art as halos from time immemorial. She was ready.

James smiled reassuringly at her as he turned his chair towards her with the opening question designed to set her at ease.

"So, Doctor Griffiths ... ..."

This really did throw her right off track, because apart from her proud parents practising with her newly awarded title when she was first awarded her doctorate, no one else had ever used *Doctor* to address her. She needed to pull herself back to the question after her humble soul registered that she was indeed entitled to the title. Her cognitive, fun brain was also processing that odd expression for a second too long- *entitled to the title*- mmm. *Not allowed to giggle doesn't look professional!*

She re focussed on James's handsome face in time to hear the end of the question.

" ... ... to study such an esoteric and may I say somewhat whimsical subject?"

Georgina smiled and cleared her throat simultaneously to give herself thinking time. She felt the warm encouragement of Lyre's smile, who knew exactly how her young friend was feeling, right then, under the studio lights and the gaze of at least one hundred people in the audience. She dare not even consider the millions watching around the world by satellite signal.

"Well, firstly, I would like to discuss your use of *esoteric* and *whimsical* in the question, James, as it is perhaps symptomatic of what led me to study energies in a more scientific way without denying the spiritual aspects that have long been derided in modern society. You see as an adjective *'esoteric'* does mean a topic that is only likely to be understood by a limited number of people with specialised knowledge, so far so good." She paused for effect to give him a smiling glare. "However when people combine esoteric with terms, as they often do, such as 'whimsical', or spooky, whacky etc - then we have a subtle indoctrination of society that leads many away from intelligent investigation. When we know that whimsical pertains to things of a fanciful, capricious even playful manner, then we cannot expect a topic to be regarded as having any serious or useful contribution to make can we? Am I right?"

Her raised chin and tight smile unsettled him.

"Whoah there Doc! I didn't mean to make you so defensive so soon, I do apologise for any offence given, but yes I suppose you are quite correct in your assessment of the way we use such language to demean a topic without even realising that we are doing it." A voice from the audience could be heard calling out "too right!" It sounded suspiciously like Freda to Lyre'e ears.

Jack and Phoebe in the control booth could not spot the right audience area to have a camera cut away in time to catch the culprit. Georgina carried on regardless;

"I am not in the least bit defensive I can assure you, but if you look more carefully into my thesis, you will see that is exactly the way language has been used semantically through the ages to discredit those who understand more of what goes on in other dimensions and also even just acknowledge and understand our own electromagnetic fields on this earth in broad daylight." She opened her arms, palms upwards, to illustrate this light energy all around them. "We all know that we are breathing in oxygen and giving out carbon dioxide, *because we have been told it is so*! Then tell me how we explain this to children, similarly when they ask us where is the wind that they can *feel* with their skin but not *see* with their eyes. We accept such things as fact and in the same way we accept that which we continually hear and then we are indoctrinated without questioning."

James was nodding in what he hoped was a placatory manner to keep her going.

"I can give you a simple example that took me several years to understand but it had worked without my realising. Over many years my own sister in law tried to discredit me with my brother by continually referring to me as 'Mystic Meg' when talking to my brother. It began as a joke (I like to think anyway) but it became progressively worse until she was permanently labelling me as ' your silly sister'. My brother in turn accepted that there was something not quite right with me and childish teasing became an almost sinister scoffing at my every word. This was all because I chose to discuss energy fields and their influence on our daily lives. I fully understood that she didn't like my acknowledging angels as an energy force either, because many have labelled such assumedly religious concepts as fantasy in spite of their being described by religious and non religious cultures across the world for centuries. It took me a while to realise that it was basic fear of the concepts that were only really being studied by physicists and in secret at that, in those days."

Lyre was nodding to encourage Georgina's enthusiastic passion for her subject. James was looking a bit hot under the collar and Eoin was bouncing up and down as he silently applauded her opening answer.

"So what I understand from all of this Dr Griffiths is that you wanted to change public awareness of the world of the energy field that is part not only of the human soul but also angels and spooks by researching and verifying what was happening across the world?"

"Please call me Georgina ..." She was aware that she had riled him already by the early challenge to his style of questioning when he had thought he was being gentle.

"Yes I wanted, want, I should, say to allow the general public, everyone, to give people permission to believe in the living energy field, the soul or spirit that does not die when the physical body stops functioning."

"Why do you say that they need permission?"

"For exactly the reasons that we have been discussing. There is an inherent fear that someone will be labelled as stupid, silly, or unintelligent if they decide to talk about the fact, yes fact, that our consciousness doesn't die - you can call it soul, spirit, consciousness or whatever makes you happy but the fact is that the basic energy of a living organism continues long after the physical entity has died. Modern Physicists are illustrating this all the time. I really do not see why it is considered controversial to say this when it is easily backed up with evidence." Georgina was on a roll now and her voice became stronger and her passion was obvious to the room.

James turned towards Lyre for his next question.

"How do you feel about such strong and controversial statements Dr Papakostas, is the world ready for this discussion presented as scientific fact?"

"Oh they're not *presented as* - they *are* factual James. Please call me Lyre, everyone does and I am of course delighted that Georgina has been allowed to write her thesis on such a broad and virtually academically ignored subject. The timeless question posed across the world of whether life exists after death has been skirted around and derided as unfit to discuss for generations. It is not so long ago that clairvoyants, mediums and healers were locked up. Indeed they were executed in the middle ages. More recently professional reputations were destroyed when experiments were planned to investigate the existence of an afterlife. So many of my own colleagues from medical school have cutely labelled me just as Georgina has described. But you see it is *me* that the patients come to when chemically based traditional western medicine has let them down. They come to me even, I need to add quite honestly, after they have been let down by bogus healers. I am willing to listen, look them in the eye and promise nothing apart from allowing them to believe, yes giving them permission, to believe in themselves. I also allow them to feel the energy of their own body as it can be mixed with the other energies of the environment. We can pollute our own electromagnetic field with all kinds of environmental energies that we do not need to function properly." James raised one well practised quizzical eyebrow at her remarks. "Yes even the energy of another person can change our own energy field if they get too close or project their feelings onto us. Each individual in our world has the ability to influence our auric field. Once they feel this energy field for themselves they know that there is so much more out there for them to work with and of course to understand."

Eoin was ecstatic right now, floating happily towards the beams in the ceiling that was holding the lights and Thomas. They did a bizarre, spirit equivalent of a high five as they met with a clash of electromagnetic atoms causing one spot to flicker momentarily.

"Oops better not do that again old boy, they're only getting started!"

Georgina, aware of the flickering spotlight was continuing the discussion after several other questions about whether such phenomena could be proved as nothing was visible or measurable. "In lay man's terms we can think about how we feel when we get home from a heavy day's work with many angry people in an office or we sit beside a particularly bad tempered person on public transport. You know how you feel if you enter a room where someone has had a huge row?" Several heads in the audience were nodding and nudges were being exchanged knowingly.

"Exactly, we allow ourselves to *feel* that energy, we accept it comes from the energy fields of other people. But we cannot see it unless we have attuned ourselves to being more present in that electromagnetic sensory area. Real clairvoyants are just the same as you but they have either never lost their ability to see and feel living energy or they have learned to re attune to the sensory perceptions that we are born with and then lose because society dictates the norm." She turned once more to Lyre and asked her friend, "Perhaps you could explain why those who have understood and seen this energy have been discredited on a professional level Lyre?"

Lyre cleared her throat to say

"It has been easy to discredit those who have real knowledge and skill because of those who have used a little learning and tried to fool the vulnerable and needy. Most of us will have met a charlatan at some time who has learned to use the terminology or spiritual jargon you could say. Perhaps they have read a couple of books and discovered a way to earn quick money by bluffing. I recently heard the expression to describe self opinionated healers as NAGGs (New Age Gossiping Gurus). I like it. Pardon the expression, James but really it is true that *bullshit baffles brains!* I say it in that way to get the point across that we all want an easy answer or quick fix to an ailment and if someone comes along offering to cure us of some ailment with their hands or tell us what our dead granny is saying we *want* to believe them. The intelligent trick lies in being discerning, being intuitive, using your own common sense. If it does not feel right to you then it is not right for you."

She looked around the room to acknowledge the muttering amongst the audience. "However we also need to be aware of what Georgina was saying about electromagnetic fields being real. Understanding basic physics is not difficult, energy is the basis of all life. What you need to do is ask the questions. If you are willing to allow someone calling themselves a *healer* to put their hands on your body then you have a right to know who they are and where they learned how to do what they do for you. I have treated some patients who have had parts of their body manipulated by lay people with no basic knowledge of the underlying human physiology, people who have no idea of how the body works under the skin. Now I think we need some professional control here, even a certificate in first aid requires knowledge of human biology. But I can also say there are some highly skilled lay healers who do not have knowledge of anything other than the energy system flowing through the body. An early example of this was discussed in Georgina's chapter about ancient Chinese medicine. Chinese practitioners can be the most skilled at working with the body's meridian lines and they study human physiology, in depth, to a high professional level, it was not always so and yet results were achieved nonetheless. This is back to my favourite mantra that you must use *your own* intuition. Do not just trust anyone whether they have an *ology* or not!" Lyre smiled at the audience as they laughed along with her use of the term made famous by Maureen

Lipman in an old television advertisement. She patted Georgina's knee to encourage her to continue the discussion.

"Laughter has always been used to cover our fears. We tend to forget that the flat earth supporters didn't believe that the world was round because they couldn't see the edge. They were certain that sailors would drop off the edge one day." The audience tittered amongst themselves. "Oh yes you laugh now but that was the popular opinion of the time. Can you imagine Heinrich Hertz looking at our use of the internet and radio waves today? He, himself, didn't even realise the practical importance of his experiments towards our future use of radio waves and electricity. He boldly stated that his research was of no use whatsoever that it was just an experiment that showed these mysterious electromagnetic waves that cannot be seen with the naked eye. *But they are there.*" She stopped to look around allowing this fact to sink in once more.

"The fact that many of his peers actively resisted his work on electricity and magnetism only further shows that professional jealousies and intransigence have historically prevented many non visible phenomena from being studied properly for the good of mankind."

Eoin was expanding on this topic in the rafters to Thomas and several angels who were watching with interest.

"Good chap old Heinrich I met him, you know, in Berlin, when he was studying under Helmholtz and Kirchoff. Must have been around 1879 just before he graduated. It was a few years before he started that pioneering stuff on electromagnetic waves, shame he died so young!" The suspended angelic audience hardly dared to ask what exactly Eoin was doing or which persona he inhabited in Germany in those days. He was looking quite nostalgic and needed to regroup his glowing aura to refocus onto the scene below.

On the studio floor the discussion had moved onto past life regression (PLRT) as a therapy. Georgina was in full flow.

"I was quite amazed when interviewing patients after they had been through regression sessions in hypnotherapy and deep meditation. The fact that eminent psychiatrists like the American Dr Weiss, were willing to believe that the person really had seen and identified themselves in many other lives was powerful evidence of the soul's journey continuing into other reincarnations you see? It has been written about for many years now, but still we hear the old rhetoric that there is no evidence, they said the same about Holtz and his electromagnetic experiments."

Eoin was doing one of his nodding energy nudges to indicate "told you so" to his etheric audience on high.

"Ok, but how does the therapist delineate between fact and fantasy when they listen to the so called other lives being described?"

"I asked that too, as part of objective research and the same answer came from all who practise that technique in hypnotherapy. They say that they don't need to differentiate or over analyse when they watch an improvement in symptoms after someone has explored a past life. If it is fantasy then it wouldn't work but acknowledging a long term pain or symptom brought in from old lives and letting it go seems to be the key to better health. I have seen chronic conditions disappear after one or two sessions with a skilled therapist."

Several voices from the audience interrupted the show, resonating with more heckles from around the room.

"What utter tosh!"

"Nonsense!"

"Baloney, yeah my granny was my dad ha ha."

"Ok ladies and gentlemen, you will get your chance to ask questions shortly, but first please let the ladies finish their contributions, if you don't mind!" James was looking stern and in command from his presenter's chair.

Lyre smiled serenely as she scanned the audience and then back to James.

"You see James this suggests that the general opinion is that all of those people who write and speak about personal near death experiences or past lives full of factual information are lying or fantasising, I mean why would they do that for a start? Eminent scientists and well educated people have spoken publicly about their personal experiences on the operating table, under hypnosis and some even during diagnosed heart attacks. You know we are all suffering from a terminal disease- it's called *life*." A few giggles could be heard from the audience at this lighter tone in Lyre's voice.

"The problem is that we don't know what we don't know ... ... If you see where I am going with this? Fear is a big motivator and fear of the fear motivates people to rail against anything that they do not or cannot easily understand...."

"Waffle;

"Academic, crap ... ...!"

James looked towards the audience as Lyre said

"Please allow them to ask the questions and then perhaps we can clarify some of this so called waffle for the last gentleman who spoke?" She turned once more towards the audience with a smile of welcome.

"How can we help with your queries sir?"

A new voice cut into the discussion. It was well modulated with a clipped English accent suggesting a high level of education.

"There is not a shred of scientific evidence for anything that you have said so far."

Once more James interjected ;

"Thank you for that Dr Fritz Keister, we know that you are a renowned cynic and researcher in this area is that correct?"

"Yes, James, I have studied para psychology, behavioural outcomes after contact with spiritual and religious zealots over many years. There are several well designed, expertly written, double blind experiments that have sought to verify most of what these ladies are saying. I am happy to state that of course the *scientific* experiments show that there has to be auto suggestion on many levels. There is always a cultural overlay to people's beliefs and interpretations as we know." Oh and it's *Professor* Keister, although you can of course call me Fritz." He leaned back pompously with his arms folded and what Georgina was later to describe as a very smug smile on his pale, rather drawn face.

Eoin was commenting in the rafters that the bold professor really ought to get outside more before he started to look even more like the spiritual energies who's existence he continually denied. The resulting angelic giggles on high seemed to add a shivery energy to the audience. More than one person was seen to shiver their shoulders as though touched by a warm air. A slightly rotund man in the front row was feeling chilly rather than warmed. He shuddered as he leaned forward to look at Fritz, one of his heroes from the magasines published to debunk anything not visible to the human eye.

Lyre greeted him with her own warm and open smile, "Hello Fritz, good to see you here. I do so value your contributions as I know that you, like myself, are not happy to accept blind religious faith or partial scientific explanations for any of the new perspectives that are really changing our assumptions about life and living phenomena today. I admire the way that you have devoted so much time to researching the inconsistencies and anomalies that govern the scientific tenets for many years gone by. However you and I both know that much academic study in science, religious and philosophical areas has been historically based *and* biased by more than methodology. Why?" She turned to embrace James and the audience with her warm gaze,

"Because all the studies are carried out by *people*, living breathing individuals, each with their own inherent bias, cultural beliefs and experience, as Fritz rightly says. All are brought into the study, no matter who carries out the research. What can we call such objectivity in this case? I don't think that it is possible to be truly objective about one's own out of body or near death experience do you?"

As Fritz Keister gathered his thoughts to wheel out his stock reply on his favourite subject of how delusional people were because of hallucinations, brain chemicals and oxygen levels affecting their reasoning. But he stopped as he realised that James had suddenly turned to look at Georgina who was starting to look decidedly dreamy with her head inclined to one side.

Fritz was starting to feel professionally slighted. He had been planning his speech since the programme began. How he disliked what he considered time being wasted by such presentations, most particularly by women. Societal bias dictated, in his mind at least, that spirits, clairvoyants and crystal balls were the domain of middle aged and elderly women with blue rinses. The fact that this programme was being dominated by two attractive *normal* looking women of different ages who, he had to subconsciously admit, had made some credible points was seriously getting to him. He could feel a guy a few seats along the row getting agitated and he hoped he would be an ally to his own counter arguments.

Georgina appeared to be gazing intently, but with a glazed look in her eyes, towards this particular guy who Fritz was starting to think about for different reasons. The short stout man on the front row of the audience, near professor Keister was a well dressed member of the audience. He had been sitting patiently waiting his turn, as a member of the humanist group invited by Jack to heckle anything that may sound like it had "god" involved as a fact. He was now loosening his sober grey tie with one hand whilst undoing the buttons of his suit jacket with the other. He had been wondering for a few minutes previously just what he had done to attract the attention of the pretty young woman on stage.

As James coughed to try to gain Georgina's attention she started to talk, apparently addressing the chubby man, in that dreamy voice he found so sexy.

"What do you want, what's happened, how did you get here?" She was starting to look quite unlike herself as she stood up to continue speaking. The guy started a stuttering reply "W'eeell I c came b b by bus …" until Lyre raised her hand indicating that he should be silent.

"It's alright sir, she is not addressing you. There is a spiritual energy immediately above you that needs to be heard. Just relax everyone as this does look very important and unprecedented, even to me." She was leaning forward on the sofa apparently also focussing on the area around chubby man who immediately shot out of his seat to collapse against the stage. He slumped to a seated position on the edge of the low stage to allow himself to look back at his recently vacated seat. The look of panic in his eyes was evident to all of the audience that he now faced.

"What! Oh no, Oh gosh, what happened to you Eddie, how did you get here?"

The rafters were really buzzing now like an ancient sailing ship, as Eoin addressed his angelic colleagues once more

"Well shiver me timbers lads here we go, the cats amongst the pigeons now, or should I say the spirit has risen, let's see how we can help!"

Kyrie screamed from a few rows back and Ralph threw his arms around her.

"She said Eddie, didn't she? Jesus!"

The scoffs and disbelief within the room were tangible.

"Clever way to avoid more questions, yeah right!"

Others started to feel uneasy as they were looking in amazement at the sweating, shaking chubby man now adorning the edge of the stage. Georgina was oblivious and still looking outwards to the spot where she continued to speak to Eddie. Her slender form and shining blonde hair gave her an almost angelic aura as her serenity balanced the sweaty, shaking man sitting in front of her.

"You're in spirit, Eddie, speak to me, you must know that you have passed over right now, don't you?" James breathed deeply and wondered how he could handle this situation. Jack was getting really excited in the booth and wondering what he could do to capitalise on this unique situation.

As it happened they did not need to worry about anything. The universe was really conspiring to change more ideas than they or their crew could ever conceive.

Chapter 18

More Light than Planned

The studio audience was buzzing with excited energy. Not all of it helpful to the subject. Eoin was smiling enigmatically now as he floated towards the distressed spirit that was Eddie somewhere above the front row.

"Spoofers,!"

"Weirdos!"

"How well orchestrated was that then eh?" The audience cynics recovered their balance quickly, clearly suspecting a set up publicity stunt. James was standing with arms outstretched patting his hands towards the audience in a placatory manner.

"Please stay calm ladies and gentlemen, whilst we see if we can unravel and verify some of this quite startling information. I can assure you this was not planned in any way."

A studio runner had her arm around the chubby man who had vacated his seat so rapidly. He was wiping his face and neck with one of the proffered tissues and still searching the vacated seat for what he hoped to see whilst he shivered and flicked his shoulders with the other hand. He knew that something was happening to his own energy field as he had felt the chill breeze wrap around him earlier. He had been watching Georgina's facial expression for a few minutes prior to the outburst. It had been fascinating to watch as her head inclined to one side, her eyes had become very dreamy and unfocussed whilst she stroked her chin gently as though feeling a goatee beard. He almost could believe that she had evolved into a Chinese man, or as he later reported "a little mandarin guy." Georgina was still using her dreamy eyed out of focus expression to listen to Eddie. He had at last managed to speak back to her. His invisible presence could clearly be seen by both her and Lyre from their positions on the low stage.

"So I am dead ... I was murdered then ... I really was, ... the bastards!" Georgina was trying to calm his spirit with her mind energy, projecting herself as far as she could into his soul energy.

"How were you murdered Eddie?" There was a gasp from the audience and another sob from Kyrie.

"Tell them please Georgie, I didn't do it. I must let Kyrie know that I have been clean since you worked with me a few months back. She must know I would never have done anything else to myself with that muck. *You* know too, I just couldn't do any more of the stuff."

"Of course they know dear boy, don't fret all will be well, you have come to the right place, in fact it couldn't have worked out better. How wonderful is this universe? It really is, I'm warming to the twenty first century after all." Eoin was excitedly attempting to blend a little of his energy with the newly disembodied Eddie.

"Who the hell are you, oh shit, I really am dead aren't I?"

"Now, now cariad, don't be speaking to Eoin like that, it is just not a good idea when we're trying to help you." Thomas floated down to flank Eddie's now shaking soul energy.

"No, I don't like this, I'm scared shitless, bugger, what the hell is happening here, and who are you for Christ's sake? How do *you* know I'm Welsh anyway?""

"*Were* Welsh dear boy, *were* being the operative word right now." Grinned Eoin as he tried once more to infiltrate Eddie's electromagnetic field that was seriously wobbling and fading rapidly in and out of the atmosphere.

"Just let me feed you a little light, for now. We'll soon have you off on your journey, you will get chance to stay here for just a few minutes until you are reassured that Georgina will get your message delivered and justice will be done, don't fret now or you will disappear along that light tunnel before you hear the good news, best get it completed now rather than come back later."

It was obvious to even the most cynical audience members that Georgina was now addressing more than one soul somewhere above the front row.

"Oh Thomas, Eoin, please don't be hard on poor Eddie, look at him he must have just passed over in the last few hours, you will be fine Eddie, has anyone come to meet you yet?"

"What? I don't know what you mean, meet me?"

Thomas was pleased to be able to add some useful information to the situation. "She means that when your body dies your soul usually gets to meet someone from the other side ...."

"*Our* side dear boy" interjected Eoin cheerfully.

"Yes," continued Thomas, like a relative, friend or grandma or some such person who has known you well and can reassure you to help you pass over in a peaceful way. Kids even get met by Father Christmas sometimes. But you don't look too peaceful right now so I suspect not, am I right?"

Jack was turning puce in the control booth shouting orders, sliding knobs and wondering could a camera catch whoever or whatever it was that Georgina was talking to.

"Gimme the press office, let me ask some questions, this could be bloody marvellous! See can you find anything with camera three, I don't know, smoke, light or ruddy Jesus Christ himself whatever, keep scanning the audience and her field of vision!"

James was listening to Jack screaming into his ear,

"Just let it roll, don't interfere unless someone gets violent, We'll try to cover all the interactions between all of the cameras. Stanley, get another roving mike down there quick. Camera 4 are you on the floor, where the hell are you? Get some closeups on the women, can *anyone* tell me who the fuck they're talking to?"

Oblivious to all of this off set activity Georgina and Lyre were working calmly together with Eoin and Thomas, trying to settle Eddie's spiritual energy in one place so that they could decipher what he so obviously needed to say. A very big angel had also zoomed in from another dimension and was almost swaddling the three spirits above the front row.

"Well done, Chamuel, we needed some angelic assistance to keep this soul stable for now. Thank you for coming, just keep those feathers out of my nose, ok?"

Chamuel smiled at Eoin, beaming his beautiful light that seemed to swamp the entire room, in so doing heating up, even more, the poor wee chubby guy who was totally in awe all of this activity.

"Now Eddie just stay calm and tell us what it is you need to say please, speak slowly and clearly because you may have only a few minutes in this dimension before you need to go." Lyre was speaking in her professional soothing tone, hoping to keep him steady.

"I have been doped that's what happened. I was sitting watching the telly in the middle of the afternoon, was working last night see, and about to switch off for a doze when my front door was kicked in. These two heavies bounded across the room at me, one pinned me down and the other stuck a ruddy great needle into my arm, couldn't do a ruddy thing. I felt it hit my brain within seconds, could almost smell it, like an anaesthetic, after being clean for so many months I had no resistance at all - whop, straight into me and then I passed out. When I came to I was up on the bloody ceiling so I was, funny thing was I didn't realise I was outside my body for a wee while like, just didn't register you know?"

Georgina was paraphrasing what he said for the benefit of the audience, exactly as Eoin had told her to. He was chortling with glee at how opportune poor Eddie's demise had been.

Lyre continued to do the questioning as Georgina reported the answers, the team work could not have been better as they all agreed when they eventually had time to discuss the evening's events.

The audience were just buzzing with excitement, a mixture of disbelief and avid curiosity. Fritz Keister was turning as puce as Jack for different reasons, Eoin took time to remark that he could see the man did have some blood in him after all.

"Why would anyone want to do this to you Eddie, do you know?" Jack was jumping up and down in the booth, shouting into James' ear piece again. "Tell the bloody woman to ask his surname for God's sake, ask her, hurry up!" James leaned towards Lyre to whisper the request in her ear. She nodded with understanding and continued her questions un phased. Eddie was chattering away to her from his soul energy.

"I sort of forgot a debt I owed to Tom, the Yank, a dealer, from away back. I had said I would pay when I got into my new job, but the weeks ran by and I really did forget 'cos I was so happy just being clean and straight. Your work with me Georgie, it really just made staying clean so simple, I was happy to be alive again for the first time in years ... Christ, now look at me ..." At this revelation he just burst into sobs at the farcical statement he had made, he had been drug free for such a short time and his whole soul was wracking with grief as he said these words.

"Just to clarify for us Eddie, you are Eddie Gethin, right? Ex Welsh guardsman and now adopted as a London, well Bromley, resident, is that correct.?" Lyre made the statement that Jack was waiting for, he had his hand on the phone immediately to ring the police to see could he corroborate any of this bizarre scenario in his studio.

"Don't worry," continued Georgina, "all is going to be as it should be. Remember we discussed universal law and energy fields in our therapy sessions? Your greatest journey is now going to begin, all will become clearer when your guide comes to take you over. You have been granted a great privilege by being allowed to come here and get this off your chest and seek appropriate action for those responsible for your death." Eoin was grinning yet again as he whispered to Chamuel that there didn't appear to be too much chest left as they were having great difficulty in sustaining his energy field in this dimension. Chamuel shushed him gently with his warm breath that seemed to come from nowhere. Below them chubby man was wondering why he could smell roses, or was it magnolia, he wasn't too sure.

"Best ask him what this Yank guy looked like Lyre darling and what he was wearing when he stuck the needle in. Just for verification when the fuzz arrive!"

Thomas choked into the ether when he heard this use of "fuzz" to describe the police force. Sometimes Eoin could be just too much.

On stage, Georgina was reporting the descriptions from Eddie about the colour of Yank Tom the Yank's hair, his jacket and a distinctive tiger tattoo that he had on the back of his hand. He also managed to describe the bigger man who had held him down. In the control booth

Jack was in seventh heaven. "Please let all of this be true, dear God I will be a believer for ever, I really will, just let it be true and told first here on my show, yeah!"

Phoebe looked over at his enthusiasm, shrugged her shoulders and dryly remarked

"Very devout."

Suddenly Eddie looked across at James on the stage and realised that his Aunt Elsie who had died in the Neath Hospital a few years ago was actually sitting on the chair that James had vacated to stand beside Georgina. She was smiling serenely at him. He had last seen her in Port Talbot smiling, in just the same way, as she thanked him for her birthday flowers. She had been 98 at the time and living in a beautiful care home, all sweeping driveways and red brick facades. The fact that she had Alzheimer's back then seemed to be all forgotten, she was waving at him enthusiastically.

"Looks like it's time to go now dear boy, your Auntie is here for you. She is a really happy soul. I met her just after she came over, what a character she is." Eoin was withdrawing his energy from Eddie's auric field as he gently sent some loving feelings into his soul. Eddie had calmed down now, knowing that he had said most of what he had been allowed the time to say. Thomas, too, was emanating pure love into the fading energy field that had been Eddie. He looked at Chamuel who was enveloping Eddie in a light field of enormous vibrational energy as Aunt Elsie floated over towards them.

"Tell me Mam I loved her, tell her I'm sorry I didn't always let her know where I was ..." The granny's in the audience were dabbing their tears right about then and tough men were gulping into their adam's apples.

"And Kyrie bach, I really did love you," Kyrie was still sobbing in the arms of Ralph and trying to see what Georgie could see over his shoulder.

"I'm so sorry I screwed up, enjoy your life thanks for all the help .... I ... just want ... " The voice trailed off as his energy field was almost dissolved into the energy that had been his Aunt and the massive Angelic sphere of Chamuel. Together they looked like a pink tinged white glow as the massive orb of light floated skywards.

Those who were more relaxed as a result of attending their regular yoga or meditation classes could actually hear a high pitched fizzing sound percolating around the studio walls. They could clearly see the light filled ceiling changing into a sparkling pink glow. There was an almost touchable stillness vibrating around everyone on the room. The luckier people could feel it. The dedicated skeptics were trying not to.

Police sirens could be heard outside the television studio as this energy filled scene was coming to an end in a now electrically charged and amazingly eerie stunned atmosphere. Georgina was still recounting what was happening into her microphone and she even managed to describe the smiling Aunt Elsie as she moved into the central energy area. She didn't really need to describe the etheric atmosphere with the pink glow that was disappearing towards the ceiling, causing all the lights and beams to vibrate as they short circuited with pyrotechnic flashes due to the cosmic interference. Short fat man from the front row was still slumped in a mass of sweaty, red faced amazement. He was visibly shaking in a state of shock, having been in full receipt of the biggest energy field he would ever experience until his own death many years later. He was already wondering how to describe the vibrational force he had experienced and the enigmatic facial expressions of both Georgina and Lyre.

Fritz Keister was frantically planning how he could refute what he would have to describe as *circumstantial, unverifiable circumstances* for his next article on Skeptics and Cynics United, The Blog

James was alongside Georgina now with a comforting arm around her shoulders, as much for his own comfort as hers. He still was not too sure what exactly he had witnessed in the studio tonight. He did know, though, that he was going to enjoy getting a complete analysis from Georgina when they eventually sat down for that glass of wine sooner rather than later. He was fast becoming aware of just how a spiritual presence can raise more than adrenaline in the human body.

The audience were still eerily quiet and most were smiling without knowing why as some dabbed tears and the floor crew rushed around dishing out tissues like an edition of the Jeremy Kyle show.

Lyre was still smiling serenely as Eoin's energy joined hers and together they waved goodbye to Eddie and Aunt Elsie, knowing that he was as yet unaware that he had helped to make history tonight. Life on earth would never be the same again by the time each member of the audience had been interviewed, by police and press, the emails had been sifted and the callers on the jammed switch board had been placated.

Jack was just happy as he put up the end credits whilst instructing cameras to pan the whole scene with sound effects of police sirens that he thought were an impressive final touch. He was scratching his head as he wondered what more he was allowed to say, the C.I.D. officer who entered the control booth helped him out.

At the end of the credits for this ground breaking discussion programme Jack was able to type:

Scotland Yard have just confirmed that a 38 year old Welsh ex soldier was found dead in his Bromley home. His next of kin have been told and the cause of death has not yet been established.

The Indigo group comprised of Lyre, Georgina, Eoin, Thomas, and occasionally Aramantha were being heard at last.

And Georgina was still only 33.

It was just the beginning for the Indigo group's influence on the world. Was the world ready for them?

The True Indigo 33

Coming soon: Indigo 34 and Indigo 35, The special group of friends from different dimensions and time zones are sought out by the most unusual people to help in even more unusual dilemmas. Murder and mayhem with a magic touch ... ...

There can be unexplained magic in the twenty first century.

Watch this etheric space ...

Also coming sooner rather than later : Susan's next self help book "The Cosmic Condom" covers the history of electromagnetic fields and scientifically spiritual methods to protect your own energy field in everyday life.

For the next editions register with www.susanphoenix.com

Acknowledgement

Many people contributed to this book. My research over the last 20 years was assisted by some of the world's wisest old souls, some no longer on earth. They know who they are.

Rough drafts have been read, helpfully criticised and corrected by:

My dedicated editor, my daughter Nicola Craft-Phoenix for her patience, humour and love.

Line Lyster of redlinecompany.com a good friend and "adopted" daughter.

Sheena and Erin Phoenix for simplifying my cover blurb into readable words.

June Smith and Lady for loyal friendship and encouraging me to keep at it when the spirit was low.

Marina Housley for allowing me to use and abuse her very special cover photograph.

Patricia Swanston a friend for being there from my first workshops in Gibraltar and Spain.

David and Dawn Ratcliffe Feterston for serious critique of my clairvoyant/mediumship sections.

Pippa and the Diamonds meditation/ healing group, Margaret, Sandra, Marina and Pat, who have sustained me through thick and thin (mostly thick!) from the Costa del Sol.

Lise Memborg-Fischer for sharing friendship, champagne and Danish love.

Mary Jane Trokell for beach walks, American style friendship, and a continuous supply of good wine just at the right time.

All workshop students who have shared their wit and wisdom so bravely.

My delightful new neighbours, Sean, Heather and George (not forgetting Merlot the dog) for their advice and technical support.

My ever loving, long suffering family of Niven, Sheena, Nicola and Bob with my beautiful grandchildren who are really fed up with hearing the phrase "I'll do that when I just get the book finished!"